'I need a passage out of here, and I need it today.' Samma swallowed. 'I could—pay something. Or I could work.'

'I already have a perfectly adequate crew. And I don't want your money.' His even glance didn't leave her face. 'So—what else can you offer?'

She gripped her hands together, hoping to disguise the fact that they were trembling.

'Last night—you asked me for a year out of my life.'

'I have not forgotten,' Roche said. 'And you reacted like an outraged nun.' The bare shoulders lifted in a negligent shrug. 'But that, of course, is your prerogative.'

'But, it's also a woman's prerogative to—change her mind.'

DEVIL AND THE DEEP SEA

BY

SARA CRAVEN

MILLS & BOON LIMITED
ETON HOUSE   18-24 PARADISE ROAD
RICHMOND   SURREY   TW9 1SR

*First published in Great Britain 1988
by Mills & Boon Limited*

© Sara Craven 1988

*Australian copyright 1988
Philippine copyright 1988
This edition 1988*

ISBN 0 263 76022 7

*Set in Plantin 11 on 11 pt.
01 – 0788 – 47272*

Typeset in Great Britain by JCL Graphics, Bristol

Made and printed in Great Britain

CHAPTER ONE

THE breeze from the sea whipped a strand of pale fair hair across Samma Briant's cheek, and she flicked it back impatiently as she bent over her drawing-board.

The waterfront at Cristoforo was crowded, as it always was when a cruise ship was in. Tourists were eagerly exploring the bars and souvenir shops along the quayside, and stopping to look at the stalls which sold locally made jewellery, carvings and paintings of island scenes. And a lot of them lingered where Samma sat on an upturned crate, amused and fascinated by her talent for capturing an instant likeness on paper, and willing to pay the modest fee she charged for her portraits.

She didn't consider herself to be an artist. She possessed a knack, no more, for fixing on some facial characteristic of each subject, and subtly exploiting it. But she enjoyed her work, and on days like this it was even reasonably lucrative.

She had a small crowd around her already, and her day would have been just about perfect, except for one large, mauve, chrome-glittering cloud on her horizon—*Sea Anemone,* surely the most vulgar motor yacht in the Caribbean, currently moored a few hundred yards away in Porto Cristo's marina. Because *Sea Anemone's* presence at Cristoforo meant that her owner, the equally large and garish Mr Hugo Baxter, would be at the hotel tonight, playing poker with Samma's stepfather, Clyde Lawson.

One glimpse of that monstrous mauve hulk lying at

anchor had been enough to start Samma's stomach churning uneasily. It was only six weeks since Hugo Baxter's last visit. She'd thought they were safe for at least another month or two. Yet, here he was again closing in for the kill, she thought bitterly, as she signed the portrait she'd just finished with a small flourish, and handed it over to her delighted sitter with a brief, professional smile.

The fact was they couldn't afford another visit from Hugo Baxter. Samma had no idea what her stepfather's exact financial position was—he would never discuss it with her—but she suspected it might be desperately precarious.

When Clyde had met and married her mother during a visit to Britain, he had been a moderately affluent businessman, owning a small but prosperous hotel, and a restaurant on the small Caribbean island of Cristoforo. The island was just beginning to take off as a cruise ship stopping-point, and the future should have been rosy—except for Clyde's predilection for gambling. While Samma's mother had been alive, he'd kept his proclivities more or less under control, but since her death two years earlier things had gone from bad to worse. The restaurant had had to be sold to pay his debts, and the hotel hadn't had the redecoration and refurbishment it needed, either.

Clyde seemed to win so seldom, Samma thought broodingly, and when Hugo Baxter was in the game his losses worsened to a frightening extent.

She motioned her next customer to the folding chair in front of her, and began to sketch in the preliminary shape of her head and shoulders with rapid, confident strokes.

Clyde's only remaining asset was the hotel. And if we lose that, she thought despondently, I'm never going to get off this island.

Probably the woman she was sketching would have thrown up her hands in horror at the thought of anyone wanting to leave Cristoforo. 'Isn't this paradise?' was the usual tourist cry.

Well, it was and it wasn't, Samma thought cynically. During the years when she'd spent her school holidays here, she'd taken the romantic view, too. She'd been in the middle of her A-level course when her mother had collapsed and died from a heart attack. She'd flown to Cristoforo for the funeral, only to discover when it was over that the trust which was paying her school fees had ceased with her mother's death, and that Clyde had no intention of paying out for her to complete her education.

'It's time you started working to keep yourself,' he told her aggressively. 'Besides, I need you here to take your mother's place.'

Sick at heart, confused by her grief for her mother, Samma had agreed to stay. But it had been a serious mistake. When Clyde had spoken of her working for her keep, he meant just that, she'd found. She received no wage for her work at the hotel. The only money she earned was through her sketches, and although she saved as much as she could towards her airfare back to the United Kingdom, it was a wretchedly slow process.

But even if she'd been reasonably affluent, she would still have been disenchanted with Cristoforo. It was a small island, socially and culturally limited, with a hideously high cost of living. And, when the holiday season ended, it was dull.

And working at the hotel, and more particularly in the small nightclub Clyde had opened in the grounds, Samma had been shocked when she'd experienced the

leering attentions of many of the male guests. Coming
from the comparative shelter of boarding-school, almost
overnight she'd discovered that to most of the male
visitors to the island she was an object, rather than a
person, and she'd been revolted by the blatant sexism of
their attitude to her. She'd soon learned to hide herself
in a shell of aloof reserve which chilled the ardour of the
most determined predator. But she was aware that, by
doing so, she was also cutting herself off from the chance
of perhaps forming a real and lasting relationship.
However, this was a risk she had to take, although she
was forced to admit she'd never been even mildly
attracted by any of the men who stayed at the hotel, or
hung round the bar at the Black Grotto club.

One day, she thought, one day, when she got back to
England and found herself a decent job, and a life of her
own, she would meet someone she could be happy with.
Until then, she'd stay insulated in her cocoon of
indifference.

Except when Hugo Baxter was around, she reminded
herself uneasily. He seemed impervious to any rebuff,
seeking her out, taking any opportunity to touch her,
Samma's skin crawled at the thought. One thing was
certain, she was keeping well away from the Black
Grotto tonight.

She handed over her completed portrait, and glanced
at her watch. It was nearly noon, and people were
drifting away in search of lunch and shade. Time for a
break, Samma thought, getting to her feet and stretching
vigorously. As she lifted her arms above her head, she
was suddenly aware she was being watched, and she
looked round.

Startled, her eyes met another gaze, dark, faintly
amused and totally male in its assessment of the thrust of
her rounded breasts against her brief cotton top,

Samma realised in the embarrassed moment before she looked away with icy disdain.

But she was left with a disturbing impression of height and strength, and sun-bronzed skin revealed by a brief pair of cut-off denims. As well as an absurd feeling of self-consciousness, she thought resentfully.

She should be used to being looked at. In a community where most people were dark-haired and dark-skinned, her pale skin and blonde hair, as straight and shining as rain water, naturally attracted attention, and usually she could cope with this.

But there had been something so provocatively and deliberately—masculine about this stranger's regard that it had flicked her on the raw.

And her antennae told her that he was still looking. She picked up her sketch-block, and began drawing at random—the neighbouring stall, where Mindy, its owner, was selling a view of the marina to a tourist couple who were trying and failing to beat him down over the price. But her fingers, inexplicably, were all thumbs, fudging the lines, and she tore the sheet off, crumpling it irritably.

She stole a sideways glance under her lashes, making an assessment of her own. He was leaning on the rail of one of the sleekest and glossiest of the many craft in the marina, and looking totally out of place, she decided critically, although she supposed he was good-looking, in a disreputable way—that was, if you liked over-long and untidy black hair, and a great beak of a nose which looked as if it had been broken at least once in its career.

He was the image, she thought contemptuously, of some old-time pirate chief, surveying the captive maiden from his quarter-deck. He only needed a cutlass and a parrot—and she would give them to him!

Her mouth curving, she drew the preliminary outline, emphasising the stranger's nose almost to the point of caricature, adding extra rakishness with earrings, and a bandanna swathed round that shock of dark hair. She transformed his expression of faint amusement into an evil leer, gave the parrot on his shoulder a squint, then pinned the sketch up on the display board behind her with a flourish.

He would never see it, of course. The boat's owner had clearly left him on watch, and probably with good reason. Only a thief bent on suicide would want to tangle with a physique that tough, and shoulders that broad.

She had a quick, retentive eye for detail, but it annoyed her just the same to find how deeply his image had impressed itself on her consciousness. One eyeball-to-eyeball confrontation and a quick sideways glance, and she'd been able to draw him at once, whereas she normally allowed herself a much more searching scrutiny before she began. Yet this sketch had worked, even if it was a shade vindictive.

And, in its way, it turned out to be a good advertisement. People strolling past stopped to laugh, and stayed to be drawn themselves. They seemed to like the element of cartoon she'd incorporated, although Mindy, loping across with a slice of water melon for her, raised his brows when he saw it, and murmured, 'Friend of yours, gal?'

'Figment of my imagination,' she retorted cheerfully.

Another swift glance had revealed, to her relief, that the rail of the boat was now deserted. Doubtless he'd remembered the owner didn't pay him for standing about, eyeing up the local talent, she thought, scooping a handful of hair back from her face with a slim, suntanned hand.

She was putting the finishing touches to the portrait of a pretty redhead with amazing dimples, undoubtedly on honeymoon with the young man who watched her so adoringly, when a shadow fell across her pad.

Samma glanced up in irritation, the words 'Excuse me' freezing unspoken on her lips.

Close to, he was even more formidable. Distance had cloaked the determination of that chin, and the firm, uncompromising lines of his mouth. There was a distinct glitter, too, in those midnight-dark eyes which Samma found distinctly unnerving.

It annoyed her, too, that he was standing over her like this, putting her at a disadvantage. He was the kind of man she'd have preferred to face on equal terms—although to do so she'd probably have to stand on her crate, she thought, her mouth quirking involuntarily.

But there was no answering softness in the face of the man towering over her. He was looking past her at the display board, where the pirate drawing fluttered in the breeze.

He said, 'I have come to share the joke.' His voice was low and resonant, with the faintest trace of an accent.

'Is there one?' Samma, aware that her fingers were trembling, concentrated hard on the elaborate combination of her initials which she used as a signature, before passing over the new sketch.

'It seems so.' His voice cut coldly across the excited thanks of the young couple, as they paid and departed. 'They say it is always instructive to see oneself through the eyes of another. I am not sure I agree.'

The pirate sketch was outrageous, over the top,

totally out of order, and Samma knew that now, but
she wasn't going to apologise. He'd damned well
asked for it, staring at her like that. Mentally
undressing her, she added for good measure.

She smiled lightly, and got to her feet, hoping he'd
step back and give her room, but he didn't.

'An interesting philosophical point,' she said.
'Forgive me if I don't hang around to debate it with
you. It's time I took a break.'

'Ideal.' The brief smile which touched his lips
didn't reach his eyes. 'I was about to offer you lunch,
mademoiselle.'

So, he was French. Samma could see Mindy
listening avidly. She said, 'Thank you, but I'm not
hungry.'

She used the tone of cool, bored finality which
worked so well with the would-be Romeos at the
hotel, but its only effect on this aggravating man was
to widen his smile.

'A drink, then?'

'Thanks, but no thanks.' Samma was angrily aware
she was being baited.

'Then a tour of *Allegra*. You seemed very interested
in her earlier.'

'Then my interest has waned—sharply,' Samma
snapped. 'And maybe you should learn to take "no"
for an answer.'

He shrugged. His skin was like teak, she noticed
irrelevantly, darkened even further by the shadowing
of hair on the muscular chest, forearms, and long,
sinewy legs.

'Is that what a pirate would do? I think not.'

Before she could guess his intention, or make any
more to thwart him, he reached for her, his hands
clamping on her waist, hoisting her into the air, and

over his shoulder like a sack of potatoes. For a moment she was stunned, dangling there, staring down at the dusty stones of the quay; then, as he began to move, she came to furious life, struggling, kicking, pummelling the strong, smooth back with her fists.

But it was like punching reinforced concrete, and he didn't even flinch. To make matters worse, she could hear laughter and even a smattering of applause from the watchers on the quay as he walked off with her.

Mindy was her friend, but he wasn't lifting a finger to help her, and if he imagined for one moment she relished this kind of treatment then she would be happy to disillusion him, she thought, almost incandescent with rage and humiliation.

She saw the slats of the gangplank beneath her. She expected that he would put her down when they reached the deck, but she was wrong. With alarming effortlessness, he negotiated a companionway, and entered a big, sunny saloon. Then, at last, he lowered her to her feet.

Breathless and giddy, she confronted him. 'You bastard!' Her voice shook. 'How dare you treat me like that?'

He shrugged again. He wasn't smiling any more. 'You chose to hold me up to ridicule. You can hardly complain if I make you look a little foolish also.'

'Well, you've achieved your objective,' Samma said grimly. 'And now I'm leaving.'

'But I prefer that you stay.' His voice was soft, but it held a note which told her that he meant it. That, if she tried to leave, she would be prevented.

'I don't know what you hope to gain by this behaviour.' With an effort, she kept her voice steady.

'Nothing too devastating, *chérie*,' he drawled.

'Merely a companion to share some food and wine with me in the middle of the day.'

Samma lifted her brows. 'Do you always have to resort to strong-arm tactics when you need company? You must be desperate.'

He laughed, showing very white teeth. 'You think so?'

No, not for a moment she didn't. This man would only have to click his fingers and women would come running, but she was on the ropes in this bout, and she would say or do anything to escape.

The saloon was enormous, and luxuriously furnished, but somehow he made it seem cramped.

He was too tall, too dominating, the kind of man she would go out of her way to avoid, and she'd been mad to provoke him with the pirate sketch.

But there wasn't anything too major to worry about, she tried to assure herself. After all, his employer could return at any time, or so she supposed. And, if the going really got tough, she could always scream for Mindy.

She gave him a straight look. 'Fine—you've had your joke. Now, I'd like to get on with my life—quietly, and without hassle.'

'Later,' he said. 'Nothing happens on these islands around noon, or hadn't you noticed?'

'I should do,' Samma said tartly. 'I've lived here for long enough.'

'You are a permanent resident?' His tone held a trace of surprise. 'But you certainly weren't born here. I thought you were one of the new generation of island-hoppers, drifting from one location to the next like a butterfly—using your—talent—to buy your living.'

There was something in his voice which told

Samma he wasn't referring to her artistic gifts, such as they were, and in spite of herself she felt a hot blush burn her face.

'Well, you thought wrong,' she said grittily. 'And now we've cleared up that little misunderstanding, perhaps you'll let me go. My friends will be wondering where I am.'

He laughed out loud at that. 'Oh, I think they know—don't you?'

Samma almost ground her teeth. Why had she got involved in this kind of verbal sparring? she asked herself despairingly. Why hadn't she adopted her usual ploy of blank eyes and assumed deafness? Why had she let him get to her like this?

She said quietly, 'Look, you've made your point. Is there any need to go on—punishing me like this?'

'Punishment?' His mouth curled, drawing her unwilling attention to the sensual line of his lower lip. 'Is that how you regard the offer of a meal. The food on *Allegra* isn't that bad.'

'You know what I mean.' Her eyes met his directly.

'Yes, I know,' he acknowledged sardonically, 'So—what do you suppose you deserve for your impudence in drawing me as you did?'

'I draw what I see,' Samma flashed. 'And everything that you've said or done since has only convinced me how right I was.'

'Is that a fact?' His voice slowed to a drawl. 'So, you really think I'm a pirate.' He shrugged. 'Then it seems I need have no compunction.'

He moved towards her, purposefully, but without haste and Samma backed away, until the pressure of the long, cushioned seat which ran the length of the saloon prevented any further retreat.

'Keep away from me.' To her fury, she sounded

breathless and very young, her words more an appeal than a command.

'Make me,' he invited silkily. There was a disturbing glint in the dark eyes as he moved closer. With one hand, he pushed her gently down on the cushion, then sat beside her.

Samma's mouth was suddenly dry. For the first time she had to question her actual physical ability to scream if the situation demanded it. She wanted to look away from him, but she couldn't. It was as if she was mesmerised—like a rabbit with a snake, she thought hysterically. She tried to steady her breathing, to mentally reject the effect his proximity was having on her. She could feel prickles of sweat breaking out all over her body, allied to a strange trembling in her lower limbs, and she tensed, bewildered by the unfamiliarity of her own reactions.

His gaze travelled slowly and relentlessly down her body, and she shivered as if it was his hands which were touching her. Since her return to Cristoforo, she'd never worn a bra, considering her firm young breasts made such a restriction unnecessary. Now, as they seemed to swell and grow heavy against the thin fabric of her top, she began to wish she was encased in whalebone from head to foot—armour-plated, even.

She saw him smile, as if he'd guessed exactly what she was thinking. His eyes continued their downward journey, resting appraisingly on the curve of her hips, and the slender length of her thighs, revealed by her brief white shorts.

She had never, she thought dazedly, been made so thoroughly aware that she was female.

He said softly, 'There are many ways of taming a woman—and I am tempted. But for an impertinent child—this is altogether more appropriate.'

Before she knew what was happening, Samma found herself face downwards over his knee, suffering the unbearable indignity of half a dozen hard and practised slaps on her rear. The first was enough to drag a startled gasp from her, and she sank her teeth into her lower lip, pride forbidding her to make another sound.

Then, with appalling briskness, he set her upright again, his amused glance taking in her flushed face and watery eyes.

When she could speak, she said chokingly, 'You swine—you bloody sadist . . . '

He tutted reprovingly. 'Your language, *mademoiselle*, is as ill-advised as your sense of humour. I have taught you one lesson,' he added coldly. 'Please do not make it necessary for me to administer another.'

'I'll find out who owns this boat,' she promised huskily. 'And when I do—I'll have you fired. I'm sure your boss would be delighted to know you take advantage of his absence by—by abusing girls in his saloon.'

He stared at her for a moment, then began to laugh. 'Considering the provocation, I think he would say you had got off lightly.' He paused. 'Had you been adult, then retribution might have taken a very different form. Perhaps you should think yourself fortunate.' He gave her a swiftly measuring look. 'And perhaps, too, you should leave—before I change my mind.'

'Don't worry,' Samma said thickly. 'I'm going.'

Uncaring of the few remaining rags of dignity left to her, she half ran, half stumbled to the door, only to hear as she scrambled up the companionway to freedom, fighting angry tears, his laughter following her.

CHAPTER TWO

IF SAMMA thought her day could not possibly get any worse, she was wrong.

She'd grabbed her drawing materials and fled back to the hotel, evading the good-humouredly ribald teasing from Mindy and the others. And she was half-way home when she realised she'd still left that damned drawing pinned to the board. But wild horses wouldn't have dragged her back there to retrieve it. Mindy would throw it away with the rest of her unsold sketches at the end of the day.

And she would have to keep away from the waterfront until she could be sure that *Allegra* had sailed, even though it would mean a reduction in her small income.

Clyde was waiting for her. 'So there you are,' he said in the grumbling tone which had become the norm in the past year. 'That blasted Nina won't be in tonight, so you'll have to take her place.'

Samma was still quivering with reaction. Flatly, she said, 'No.'

His sunburned face went a deeper shade of brick-red. 'What do you mean—no?'

'Exactly what I say.' She glared back at him. 'I hate being in the club, and I won't sit with the customers and encourage them to buy expensive drinks they can't afford. It's degrading.'

'When I want your moral judgements, I'll ask for them,' Clyde snapped. 'You don't pick and choose what you do round here, and tonight you're standing in for Nina in the Grotto. It's no big deal,' he added disgustedly. 'Just sit with the punters, and be nice to them. No one's suggesting you sleep with them.'

Samma's delicate mouth curled. 'Meaning Nina doesn't?'

'That's no concern of yours,' Clyde blustered. 'Now, be a good girl,' he went on, a wheedling note entering his voice. 'And do something about your hair,' he added, giving its shining length a disparaging glance. 'Nina's left one of her cocktail dresses in the dressing-room, so you can wear that. You're near enough the same size.'

'It's not a question of size,' Samma said with irony. 'It's taste—something Nina's not conspicuous for.'

Clyde shrugged. 'Well, at least she doesn't look as if she's just stepped out of a kindergarten,' he countered brutally. 'Maybe you should ask her for a few lessons. Anyway, I haven't time to argue the toss with you. I have a busy evening ahead of me.'

She said evenly, 'Playing poker, I suppose. Clyde—couldn't you give the game a miss for once?'

'No, I couldn't,' he said sullenly. 'Baxter's here again, and he's loaded. All I need is one good win. His luck can't last for ever.'

'Can't it? Does it ever occur to you that he wins too often and too much for it to be purely luck?'

'You don't know what you're talking about,' he dismissed crossly. 'Now, get on with some work, please. And chivvy up those girls who work on the bedrooms. Number Thirty-three claims his bed was made up with a torn sheet.'

Samma sighed. 'A lot of the linen's threadbare. We need to replace it,' she began, but Clyde was already disappearing, as he invariably did when she tried to discuss anything about expenditure with him.

She sighed again, as she went into the hotel office

at the back of the reception desk. In spite of her
intentions, it seemed she had to put in an appearance
at the club that night. And it occurred to her too that
Clyde, who knew how much she hated being there,
had never pressured her quite so much before. In the
past, he'd been prepared, albeit sulkily, to accept her
excuses. Now, it seemed, they had entered on a new
phase in their uneasy working relationship, and
Samma wasn't sure how to deal with it. But it was
beginning to seem even more imperative that she
should get away from Cristoforo, and fast.

But without money, how can I? she thought
despairingly. And I can't even do my portraits for the
next few days because of that damned Frenchman.

She bit her lip. Meeting an—animal like him was
another incentive for her to get back to civilisation
without delay.

She might have behaved badly—she was prepared to
admit that, but his reaction had been unforgivable.
Clearly he was the kind of man who was unable to
overlook any slight to his self-esteem, which made
him both macho and humourless, she thought—faults
which far outweighed the overwhelming physical
attraction which she'd been unable to deny, or even
resist.

In the same way, she was unable to escape a
lingering curiosity about him. He looked tough, and
eminently capable, the typical roughneck who made a
precarious living, crewing on charter hire boats for
fair-weather sailors. But his voice had been educated,
she thought frowning, so that didn't add up.

Perhaps, like herself, he was trying to scrape
together the fare back to Europe, she decided with a
mental shrug. In the event, speculation was useless.
She would never see him again. Fortunately, the

Black Grotto kept away his sort of man, with its hefty cover charge and loaded drinks prices.

She could only wish it kept away Hugo Baxter's kind of man, too.

But that, of course, was too much to hope for, she realised some hours later, watching his plump figure make its way across the crowded club to her side, a self-satisfied smile on his full lips.

'Well, sweet Samantha.' His eyes were all over her, missing nothing, from the casual blonde top-knot into which she'd twisted her hair, to the slender, strappy sandals on her bare feet. 'You're a sight for sore eyes.' He leered at Nina's horror of a dress—black, and almost transparent, with a sprinkling of sequins to veil the wearer's breasts and form a coy band round the hips. It would take all her reserves of coolness to enable her to carry the tacky thing off with any degree of sang-froid she had thought wretchedly, viewing herself in the dressing-room mirror.

She said, 'Good evening, Mr Baxter.'

'Oh, come on, sweetheart. Why so formal? Surely you know me well enough by now to be—a little more friendly.' He paused. 'I looked for you on the quay this afternoon. Had a fancy to have my portrait drawn,' he added, as if conferring an immense honour.

'I have all the commissions I can handle,' Samma told him untruthfully. The thought of committing his unprepossessing features to paper was totally unappealing, although she knew how she would do it, she thought, a little curl of malicious glee unwinding inside her.

His face fell. 'That's too bad. So—how about a little dance with me, then?'

The prospect of being held in his arms, his paunch pressing against her slenderness, made Samma feel as if a sudden outbreak of maggots was crawling over her skin. She stepped back instinctively, aware that he'd registered her hurried recoil.

'I'm sorry——' she began, but he interrupted.

'You will be, sweetheart, if you start giving me the runaround. I'm a good customer of this club, and you're a hostess—right? And if I want to buy some of your time tonight, there isn't a damned thing you can do about it—right, too?'

'Quite right, *monsieur*, except that the lady's time this evening has already been bought—by me.'

The voice came from behind, but even without that betraying *'monsieur'* she would have recognised it anywhere.

As she swung round, she stiffened, her eyes blanking out with shock as she saw him. He must be well paid on *Allegra*—either that or he'd raided his employer's wardrobe. His lightweight suit was expensive, his open-necked shirt pure silk, and his shoes handmade. He looked like someone to be reckoned with in his own right, she thought, rather than simply another man's deckhand.

Hugo Baxter was gaping indignantly at him. 'Don't I know you from somewhere?' he demanded aggressively.

'Perhaps.' The Frenchman shrugged faintly, indicating how little it mattered. He turned to Samma, the dark eyes sweeping over her in amused and ironic comprehension. 'I am sorry I am late, *chérie.*' He ran a finger lazily and intimately down the curve of her cheek. 'It was good of you to wait for me.'

She was stranded, Samma thought hysterically, between the devil and the deep sea. She said, 'What did you expect?'

'Now that is something we could more profitably discuss over a drink.' His hand grasped her elbow, urging her away from the bar and towards a vacant table at the edge of the small dance-floor. 'But my expectations did not include this—metamorphosis,' he added, a note of unholy amusement in his voice. 'Are you sure, *mademoiselle*, you have no younger sister?'

She was sorely tempted to tell him she had, but her previous experience at his hands warned her it might be unwise to play any more games.

She said coolly, 'I don't know why or how you found your way here, but if you've come to score points, maybe I should warn you it'll cost you a week's wages, plus an arm and a leg. I should get back to the waterfront. You'll find the bars cheaper there.'

'Yes, I heard this was a clip-joint,' he said, unruffled. 'But it makes no difference. I came because poker is a favourite relaxation of mine, and I am told there is a game here tonight.'

There is.' Samma raised her eyebrows. 'But I think you'll find the other players take it rather more seriously than that.'

'They may need to.' A faint smile twisted round the corners of the firm mouth. 'So—how do you fit into this set-up?'

'My stepfather owns the hotel, and the club,' she said reluctantly. 'I help out when necessary.'

'I see.' His glance rested briefly and intimately on the flimsy sequin flowers which cupped her breasts, and Samma choked back a little gasp, thankful the club's dim lighting masked the colour rising hotly in her face.

She said tautly, 'I doubt it. Anyway, I don't have to explain myself to you, so perhaps you'll go now and leave me in peace.'

His sardonic gaze took in the crowded, smoke-filled room, where a buzz of laughing, chattering voices vied for supremacy with the band.

'This is your idea of peace, *chérie*? ' he drawled. 'I had a different impression of you this morning.'

'I remember it well,' Samma flashed. 'I still have the bruises.'

'I think you exaggerate. Besides,' he glanced towards the bar, where Hugo Baxter still glowered in their direction, 'you surely do not wish to be left to the mercies of that wolf?'

'You're so much better?' She sent him a muted glare. 'But you really don't have to bother about me. I can take care of myself. And he's not a wolf,' she added, reverting in her mind's eye to the portrait she'd planned. 'He's a pig, all pink and smooth, with a snout, and nasty little eyes half buried in fat.'

His brows rose mockingly. 'You take a scurrilous view of the rest of humanity, *mignonne*. I hope this time your picture remains in your imagination only. Mr Baxter would be even less amused than I was if he knew how you saw him.'

'So, you know who he is.' Samma remembered that brief confrontation at the bar.

'Who does not?' He lifted a shoulder. 'Both he—and his boat—tend to be unforgettable.'

Samma recalled just in time that this man was an enemy, and managed to stifle a giggle.

'Then perhaps you should know he's also a member of this poker school you're so keen to join,' she said tartly. 'And he can afford to lose a great deal more than a deckhand's wages.'

'So I believe.' He smiled faintly. 'But your concern is unnecessary.'

'I'm not concerned in the slightest,' Samma denied instantly. 'It wouldn't matter to me if you lost every cent you possessed, but you could turn out to be a sore loser,' she added, with a dubious look at the dark, tough face, and the raw strength of his shoulders.

He said softly, 'It is true I prefer to win,' and once again Samma was aware of that swift, appraising glance. She saw with relief that a waiter was approaching.

'Good evening, sir. What may I get you?' The cover charge was already noted on his pad as he waited deferentially.

'A straight Jack Daniels,' the Frenchman said, looking enquiringly at Samma. But the waiter interposed smoothly.

'And a champagne cocktail for the lady, sir?'

Her companion shrugged again, his mouth twisting derisively. 'If that is the usual practice—then by all means.'

Samma would have preferred fruit juice, but she knew protest was useless. She sat in smouldering silence until the drinks arrived, waiting vengefully for him to pick up the bill. But his face was expressionless as he glanced at the total, and it was Samma who found herself gaping, as he produced a bulging bill-fold, and peeled off the necessary amount, adding, she noticed, a tip for the waiter.

God, it was galling to find that he had all that money to waste on alcohol and gambling, when she was struggling to raise the price of an airfare to the United Kingdom! She tasted her cocktail, repressing a slight shudder. She knew that, if this man had been one of her island friends, she would have swallowed her pride, and asked for a loan.

Oh, why do friends have to be poor, and enemies

rich? she wondered bitterly.

'Well, why don't you ask me?' he said, and she bit back a startled gasp, wondering whether he included thought-reading among his other unpleasant attributes.

'Ask what?' She took another sip of her drink.

'How I make my money,' he drawled. 'Your face, *ma belle*, is most revealing. You're wondering how a humble deckhand could posibly have amassed so much money—or, if your earliest assessment is correct, and it is—pirate's loot.'

'Nothing about you, *monsieur*, would surprise me. But it isn't very wise to flaunt quite so openly the fact that you're loaded. Aren't you afraid of being ripped off?'

He said coolly, 'No.' And she had to believe him. If this man chose to keep a gold ingot as a pet, she couldn't see anyone trying to take it away from him.

He went on, 'But when I see something I want, I'm prepared to pay the full price for it.' Across the table his eyes met hers, then with cool deliberation he counted off some more money and pushed the bills across to her.

It was only to be expected, working where she was, dressed as she was, and she knew it, but she was burning all over, rage and humiliation rendering her speechless.

When she could speak, she said thickly, 'I am—not for sale.'

'And I am not in the market.' He leaned forward. 'Didn't you hear me say, *chérie*, that I'm here to play poker? No, this is payment for the sketch you did of me. I presume it is enough. Your artist friend on the quay told me your usual charges, and where I would find you.'

More than ever, she wished she'd ripped that particular sketch to pieces. 'I don't want your money.'

'Then you're no businesswoman.' His voice gentled slightly. 'Forget how much you loathe me, and take the money. You cannot afford such gestures, and you know it.'

Samma bit her lip savagely, wondering exactly how much Mindy had told him.

'I make a perfectly good living,' she said defiantly. She gestured around her. 'As you see, business is booming.'

'I see a great many things,' he said slowly. 'And I hear even more. So this is your life, Mademoiselle Samantha Briant, and you are content with it? To sketch in the sunlight by day, and at night lure the unwary to their doom in a net of smiles and blonde hair?'

No, she thought. It's not like that at all.

Aloud, she said, 'If that's how you want to put it—yes.'

'Did you never have any other ambitions?'

She was startled into candour. 'I wanted originally to teach—art, I suppose. But I haven't any qualifications.'

'You could acquire some.'

Samma's lips parted impulsively, then closed again. She'd been, she thought with concern, on the very brink of confessing her financial plight to this man.

She shrugged. 'Why should I—when I'm having such a wonderful time?' She pushed back her chair, and got to her feet. 'And you've acquired an instant portrait—not exclusive rights to my company. I'm neglecting the other customers.'

As she made to move away, his hand captured her wrist, not hurting her, but at the same time making it impossible for her to free herself. The dark eyes were unsmiling as they studied her. 'And what would a man have to pay for such rights, my little siren?'

She tried to free herself, and failed. 'More than you could afford,' she said bitingly, and he laughed.

'You estimate yourself highly, *mignonne*. I am not speaking of a lifetime's devotion, you understand, but perhaps a year out of your life. What price would you place on that?'

Something inside Samma snapped. Her free hand closed round the stem of her glass, and threw the remains of her cocktail straight at his darkly mocking face.

She could hear the sudden stillness all around them as her deed was registered at the adjoining tables, then the subdued, amused hum of interest which followed. And, out of the corner of her eye, she saw Clyde bearing down on her, bursting with righteous indignation.

'Have you taken leave of your senses?' he stormed at her, before turning deferentially to the Frenchman who was removing the worst of the moisture with an immaculate linen handkerchief.

'I can't apologise enough,' he went on. 'Naturally, we'll be happy to arrange any cleaning of your clothes which is necessary, Mr—er . . .?' He paused.

'Delacroix,' the Frenchman said. 'Roche Delacroix.'

Clyde's mouth dropped open. 'From Grand Cay?' he asked weakly, and at the affirmative nod he gave Samma an accusing glance. 'You'd better get out of here, my girl. You've done enough damage for one evening.'

'Don't be too hard on your *belle fille, monsieur,*' Roche Delacroix said. 'She has been—provoked, I confess.'

'I don't need you to fight my battles for me,' Samma

flared hardily. 'And nothing would prevail on me to stay in this place another moment.'

Her legs were shaking under her, but she managed to walk to the door, ignoring the murmured comments and speculative looks following her, then she dashed for the comparative refuge of the dressing-room.

Margot, one of the other hostesses, was in there, sharing a cigarette with Cicero the barman. They looked up in surprise as Samma came bursting in.

'What's the matter, honey?' Cicero asked teasingly. 'Devil chasing your tail?'

Samma sank down on the nearest chair. She said, 'I've done an awful thing. I—I threw a drink over a customer.'

'That old Baxter man?' Margot laughed. 'I wish I'd seen it.'

Samma gulped. 'No, it was a stranger—or nearly. I—I had a run in with him this morning, as a matter of fact.'

'That's not like you.' Margot gave her a sympathetic look. 'What do they call this man?'

Samma frowned. 'He said his name was Roche Delacroix and that he came from Grand Cay.'

There was an odd silence, and she looked up to see them both staring at her. 'Why—what is it?'

'I said the devil was chasing you,' Cicero muttered. 'It's one of those Devil Delacroixes from Lucifer's own island.'

'You—know him?' Samma asked rather dazedly.

'Not in person, honey, but everyone round here knows the Delacroix name. Why, his ancestor was the greatest pirate who ever sailed these waters. Every time he left Grand Cay, a fleet of merchant ships went to the bottom, and he didn't care whether they were

English or Spanish, or even French like himself. He'd had to leave France because he'd quarrelled with the King, which was a mighty bad thing to do in those days, and he figured the whole world was his enemy. So they called him *Le Diable,* yessir.' Cicero laughed softly. 'And they called his hideout Lucifer's Cay.'

'Did they, indeed?' Samma said grimly. 'Well, I hope they caught him and hanged him from his own yardarm.'

'Not on your life,' said Cicero. 'He turned respectable, got a free pardon, and took up sugar planting. But they say every now and then the breeding throws up another Devil—a chip off the old block, like that old pirate.'

He paused. 'This Mr Roche Delacroix now, why, they reckon he's made more money than old Devil Delacroix himself. He owns the casino, right there on Grand Cay, and he has a boat-chartering business as well. He's one rich guy, all right.'

'And he's here in this club right now?' Margot asked huskily, her full lips curving in a smile. 'This I have to see. Maybe when he's dried off, he'd like some company.'

'Perhaps—but I think he's more interested in playing poker.' Samma forced a smile. 'Maybe I should have found someone else to pour a drink over.'

'You sure should,' Cicero agreed sombrely. 'Why, honey, you don't ever want to cross anyone from Lucifer's Cay—specially someone by the name of Delacroix. That was one bad mistake.'

Margot rose, pretty and sinuous as a cat. 'Then I'll have to try and make up for it,' she said, her lips curving in an anticipatory smile. 'Wish me luck, now.'

She drifted out, and Cicero followed a moment or

two later, leaving Samma alone.

She tore off Nina's dress and bundled it back on a hanger. Never, ever again would she work at the Black Grotto in any capacity, although Clyde was unlikely even to ask her again, after tonight's performance, she reminded herself wryly.

She dragged on her T-shirt and jeans, and walked back through the grounds towards the small bungalow she shared with Clyde.

She felt restless—on edge, and it was all the fault of that foul man. In just a few hours, he'd turned the quiet backwater of her life into some kind of raging torrent, she thought resentfully.

And nothing Cicero had told her had done anything to put her mind at ease. It was no wonder Roche Delacroix had been annoyed at her sketch, she thought restively. He probably considered she knew who he was, and was taking a petty swipe at his family history.

Well, let him think what he wanted. He would be leaving soon and, anyway, his opinions were of no concern to her. Indeed, she didn't know why she was wasting a second thought on the creature.

But, at this rate, she wasn't going to sleep tonight. Some hard physical exercise was what she needed to calm her down, and tire her out. She turned down the path which led to the hotel's small swimming pool. She rarely got the chance to use the pool during the day, but that wasn't too much of a hardship when she could come down here at night, and have it all to herself. And there was the added bonus that she didn't have to bother with a costume.

She collected a towel from one of the changing cabins, stripped and plunged into the water. But, as she struck out with her swift, practised crawl, she couldn't seem to capture her usual sense of wellbeing.

Oh, it wasn't fair, she thought with a kind of desperate impatience. Of all the men who'd passed through Cristoforo, there had never been one who'd come even close to touching her emotions. Yet, in the space of a few minutes, Roche Delacroix, of all people, had given her a swift, disturbing insight into what it might mean to be a woman—even though he'd treated her for most of the time like a child, she thought stormily, as she turned for another length.

And then—paradoxically—had come that cynical —that abominable offer.

'*A year out of your life.*' His words seemed to beat a tattoo in her brain. How dared he? she raged inwardly. Oh, how dared he? And it was no comfort to tell herself that he'd simply been amusing himself at her expense. After all, a man like that could have no real interest in an inexperienced nineteen-year-old. Margot, or even the absent Nina, would be far more his type.

But soon *Allegra* would be gone, she tried to console herself, and she would never have to see Roche Delacroix or think about him again.

She hauled herself out of the water, and began to blot the moisture from her arms and body, then paused suddenly, a strange prickle of awareness alerting her nerve-endings as if—as if someone was watching her.

She stopped towelling her hair, and glanced over her shoulder, searching for a betraying movement in the shadows, listening for some sound. But there was nothing.

She was being over-imaginative, she told herself, but she still felt disturbed, and she resolved to give nude swimming a miss for a while. If one of the waiters from the club, say, was taking a short-cut through the garden, there was no need to give him a field day.

She pulled her clothes on to her still-damp body, and set off back towards the bungalow, her head high, looking neither to right or left.

Probably there was no one there at all. But everything was off-key tonight because of Roche Delacroix, and she would be eternally grateful when he turned his back on Cristoforo for ever.

Because, to her shame, she knew she would always be left wondering just what that—that year out of her life might have been like—with him.

CHAPTER THREE

SAMMA was woken from a light, unsatisfactory sleep
by a crash, and a muffled curse. She sat up, glancing
at the illuminated dial of the clock beside her bed,
whistling faintly when she saw the time. The poker
game had gone on for longer than usual.

She lay for a few moments, listening to the sounds
of movement from the kitchen, then reached
resignedly for her robe.

Clyde was sitting at the table, staring into space, a
bottle and glass in front of him. The eyes he turned on
her were glazed and bloodshot.

He muttered, 'Oh, there you are,' as if he'd been
waiting for her to join him.

She said, 'I'll make some black coffee.'

'No, sit down. I've got to talk to you.'

She said, 'If it's about what happened earlier—I'm
sorry . . .'

'Oh, that.' He made a vague, dismissive gesture.
'No, it's something else.'

He was a terrible colour, she thought uneasily.

He said, 'Tonight—I lost tonight, Samma.'

The fact that she'd been expecting such news made
it no easier to hear, she discovered.

She said steadily, 'How much?'

'A lot. More than a lot. Money I didn't have.' He
paused, and added like a death knell, 'Everything.'

Samma closed her eyes for a moment. 'The hotel?'

'That, too. It was the last game, Samma. I had the
chance to win back all that I'd lost and more. You

34

never saw anything like it. There were only the two of us left in, and he kept raising me. I had a running flush, king high. Almost the best hand you can get.'

She said in a small, wintry voice, 'Almost, but not quite it seems.'

Clyde looked like a collapsed balloon. She was afraid he was going to burst into tears. 'He had—a running flush in spades, beginning with the ace.'

There was a long silence, then Samma roused herself from the numbness which had descended on her.

She said, 'You and Hugo Baxter have been playing poker together for a long time. Surely he'll be prepared to give you time—come to some arrangement over the property . . .'

'Baxter?' he said hoarsely. 'I'm not talking about Baxter. It was the Frenchman, Delacroix.'

This time, the silence was electric. Samma's hand crept to her mouth.

She felt icy cold. 'What—what are we going to do?'

'Baxter will help us,' he said rapidly. 'He promised me he would. He—he doesn't want to see us go under. He's going to see Delacroix with me tomorrow to—work something out. He's being—very generous.'

There was something about the way he said it—the way he didn't meet her gaze.

She said, 'Why is he being so—generous? What have you promised in return. Me?'

He looked self-righteous. 'What do you take me for?'

'Shall we try pimp?' Samma said, and Clyde came out of his chair, roaring like a bull, his fists clenched. He met her calm, cold stare and subsided again.

'We—we mustn't quarrel,' he muttered. 'We have to stick by each other. Baxter—likes you, you know that. And he's lonely. It wouldn't hurt to be nice to him, that's all he wants. Why, you could probably get him to marry you . . .'

'Which would make everything all right, of course,' she said bitterly. 'Forget it, Clyde, the idea makes me sick to my stomach.'

'Samma, don't be hasty. What choice do we have? Unless Baxter supports me in some deal with Delacroix, we'll be bankrupt—not even a roof over our heads.'

She rose to her feet. 'This is your mess, Clyde,' she said. 'Don't expect me to get you out of it.'

Back in her own room, she leaned against the closed door and began to tremble like a leaf. In spite of her defiant words, she had never felt so frightened, so helpless in her life. She seemed incapable of rational thought. She wanted to cry. She wanted to be sick. She wanted to lie down on the floor, and drum with her heels, and scream at the top of her voice.

All she seemed to see in front of her was Hugo Baxter's sweating moon face, his gaze a trail of slime as it slid over her body.

No, she thought, pressing a convulsive fist against her lips. Oh God, no!

Clyde said there was no other choice, but there had to be. Had to . . .

'*A year out of your life.*' The words seemed to reverberate mockingly in her brain. '*A year out of your life.*'

She wrapped her arms round her body, shivering. No, that was unthinkable, too. She shouldn't even be allowing such an idea to enter her mind.

And yet, what could she do—caught, as she was, between the devil and the deep sea once again? But surely that didn't mean she had to sell herself to the devil?

She lay on the bed, staring into the darkness, her tired mind turning over the alternatives. She was blushing all over, as she realised exactly what she was contemplating.

But wasn't she being rather melodramatic about the whole thing? She didn't have to meekly submit to the fate being designed for her. She was no stranger, after all, to keeping men at arm's length. Surely, she could manage to hold him off at least until they reached *Allegra's* first port of call when, with luck, she could simply slip ashore and vanish, she thought feverishly. Her savings were meagre, but they would tide her over until she could find work, and save for her flight home.

She couldn't let herself think too deeply about the inevitable problems. The important thing was to escape from Cristoforo—nothing mattered more than that—before she found herself trapped into a situation with Hugo Baxter that she could not evade. Because it was clear she couldn't count on Clyde to assist her.

She began to plan. She would take the bare minimum from her scanty wardrobe—just what she could pack into her bicycle basket. And she'd leave a note for Clyde saying she was having a day on the beach to think. With luck, she would be long gone before he realised she was not coming back.

When it was daylight, she went over to the hotel, and carried out her usual early morning duties, warning the staff not to expect Clyde until later in the day. Then she collected a few belongings together, wrapped them in a towel to back up her beach story, and cycled down the quay.

Apart from the fishermen preparing to embark,

there were few people about. Samma bit her lip as she approached *Allegra's* gangplank. She wished she could have said goodbye to Mindy and the rest of her friends, but at the same time she was glad they weren't around to witness what she was doing.

'Can I help you, *ma'mselle?*' At the top of the gangway, her path was blocked very definitely by a tall coloured man, with shoulders like a American quarter-back.

She squared her shoulders, and said, with a coolness she was far from feeling, 'Would you tell Monsieur Delacroix that Samantha Briant would like to speak with him.'

The man gave her a narrow-eyed look. 'Mist' Roche ain't seeing anyone right now, *ma'mselle*. You come back in an hour or two.'

In an hour or two, her courage might have deserted her, she thought. She said with equal firmness, 'Please tell him I'm here, and I have some money for him.'

It was partly true. The small roll of bills representing her savings reposed in the pocket of her faded yellow sundress.

The man gave her another sceptical glance, and vanished. After a few minutes, he returned.

'Come with me, please.'

The companionway and the passage to the saloon were only too familiar, but she was led further along to another door, standing slightly ajar. The man tapped lightly on the woodwork, said, 'Your visitor, boss,' and disappeared back the way he'd come, leaving Samma nervously on her own.

She pushed open the door, and walked in. It was a stateroom, the first glance told her, and furnished more luxuriously than any bedroom she'd ever been in on dry land.

And in the sole berth—as wide as any double bed—was Roche Delacroix, propped up against pillows, a scatter of papers across the sheet which barely covered the lower half of his body, a tray of coffee and fruit on the fitment beside him.

Samma took a step backwards. She said nervously, 'I'm sorry—I didn't realise. I'll wait outside until you're dressed.'

'Then you will wait for some considerable time.' He didn't even look at her. His attention was fixed frowningly on the document he was scanning. 'Sit down.'

Samma perched resentfully on the edge of a thickly padded armchair. Its silky upholstery matched the other drapes in the room, she noticed. She wasn't passionately interested in interior decoration, but anything was better than having to look at him.

She thought working in the hotel would have inured her by now to encountering people in various stages of nudity, but none of their guests had ever exuded Roche Delacroix's brand of raw masculinity. Or perhaps it was the contrast between his deeply bronzed skin, and the white of the bed linen which made him look so flagrantly—undressed.

The aroma of the coffee reached her beguilingly and, in spite of herself, her small straight nose twitched, her stomach reminding her that she'd eaten and drunk nothing yet that day.

Nor, it appeared, was she to be offered anything— not even a slice of the mango he was eating with such open enjoyment.

'So—Mademoiselle Briant,' he said at last, a note of faint derision in his voice. 'Why am I honoured by this early visit? Have you come to pay your stepfather's poker debts? I am surprised he could raise such a sum so quickly.'

'Not—not exactly.' A combination of thirst and nerves had turned her mouth as dry as a desert.

His brows lifted. 'What then?'

She couldn't prevaricate, and she knew it. She said, 'I know you're leaving Cristoforo today. I came to ask you to—take me with you.'

They were the hardest words she'd ever had to utter, and they were greeted by complete silence.

He sat up, disposing his pillows more comfortably, and Samma averted her gaze in a hurry. When she glanced back, he was rearranging the sheet over his hips with cynical ostentation.

'Why should I?' he asked baldly.

'I need a passage out of here, and I need it today.' She swallowed. 'I could—pay something. Or I could work.'

'I already have a perfectly adequate crew. And I don't want your money.' His even glance didn't leave her face. 'So—what else can you offer?'

She'd been praying he would be magnanimous—let her down lightly, but she realised now it was a forlorn hope.

She gripped her hands together, hoping to disguise the fact they were trembling.

'Last night—you asked me for a year out of my life.'

'I have not forgotten,' he said. 'And you reacted like an outraged nun.' The bare, shoulders lifted in a negligent shrug. 'But that, of course, is your prerogative.'

'But, it's also a woman's prerogative to—change her mind.'

When she dared look at him again, he was pouring himself some more coffee, his face inscrutable.

At last he said, 'I assume there has been some crisis in your life which has made you favour my offer. May

I know what it is?'

She said in a small voice, 'I think you already know. My stepfather lost everything he possesses to you last night.'

'He did, indeed,' he agreed. 'Have you come to offer yourself in lieu of payment, *chérie?* If so, I am bound to tell you that you rate your rather immature charms altogether too highly.'

This was worse than she could have imagined. She said, 'He's going to pay you—everything. But he's going to borrow—from Hugo Baxter.'

'A large loan,' he said meditatively. 'And the collateral, presumably, is yourself?'

She nodded wordlessly.

'Now I understand,' he said softly. 'It becomes a choice, in fact—my bed or that of Hugo Baxter. The lesser of two evils.'

Put like that, it sounded awful, but it also happened to be the truth, she thought, gritting her teeth. 'Yes.'

'Naturally, I am flattered that your choice should have fallen on me,' the smooth voice went on relentlessly. 'But perhaps you are not the only one to have had—second thoughts. The prospect of being—doused in alcohol for the next twelve months is not an appealing one.'

'I'm sorry about that.' Her hands were clenched so tightly, the knuckles were turning white. She said raggedly, 'Please—please take me out of here. I'm—desperate.' Her voice broke. 'I'll do anything you ask—anything . . .'

'*Vraiment?*' He replaced his cup on the tray, and deftly shuffled his papers together. 'Then let us test your resolve, *mignonne.* Close the door.'

In slight bewilderment, she obeyed. Then, as she turned back, realisation dawned, and she stopped dead, staring at him in a kind of fascinated horror.

He took one of the pillows from behind him, and tossed it down at his side, moving slightly at the same time to make room for her. His arm curved across the top of the pillow in invitation and command.

'Now ?' She uttered the word as a croak.

His dark eyes glittered at her. 'What better way to begin the day?' He patted the space beside him. *'Viens, ma belle.'* He added, almost as an afterthought, 'You may leave your clothes on that chair.'

Shock held her prisoner. She couldn't deny that she'd invited this, but she hadn't expected this kind of demand so soon. Had counted, in fact, on being allowed a little leeway. Time to adjust, she thought. Time to escape . . .

'You are keeping me waiting,' his even voice reminded her.

She took a few leaden steps forward, reached the chair, and paused. She could refuse, she supposed, or beg for a breathing space. And probably find herself summarily back on the quayside with her belongings, she realised, moistening her dry lips with the tip of her tongue, as she eased her slender feet out of her espadrilles.

Her heart was beating rapidly, violently, like a drum sending out an alarm signal, a warning tattoo. She had never in her life taken off her clothes in front of a man, and she didn't know how to begin. What was he expecting? she wondered wildly. Some kind of striptease—all smiles and tantalisation? Because she couldn't—couldn't . . .

She put up a hand and tugged at the ribbon which confined her hair at the nape of her neck, jerking it loose.

He was propped on one elbow, watching her in

silence, his face enigmatic, but she had the feeling he wasn't overly impressed with her performance so far.

She supposed she couldn't blame him. He'd spelt it out for her, after all. 'My bed or that of Hugo Baxter,' he'd said. 'The lesser of two evils.' Well, she'd made her decision, and now, it seemed, she had to suffer the consequences.

She bent her head, letting her hair swing forwards to curtain her flushed face while she tried to concentrate her fumbling fingers on the buttons which fastened the front of her dress.

The sharp, imperative knock on the stateroom door was as shocking as a whiplash laid across her overburdened senses, and she jumped.

'Radio message for you, boss. Maître Giraud—and I reckon it's urgent.'

Roche Delacroix swore under his breath, and made to throw back the sheet, pausing when he encountered Samma's stricken look. He paused, his mouth twisting cynically. 'You'll find a robe in that closet, *chérie*. Get it for me.'

She hurried to obey, holding the garment out to him almost at arm's length.

He laughed. 'Now turn your back, my little Puritan.'

Heart hammering unevenly, she heard the sounds of movement, the rustle of silk as he put on the robe. But when his hands descended on her shoulders, turning her to face him again, a little cry escaped her.

'How nervous you are.' The laughter was still there in his voice. 'Like a little cat who has never known kindness.' He picked up her hand, and pressed a swift, sensuous kiss into its soft palm. 'I am desolated our time together has been interrupted, *ma belle*, but it is only a pleasure postponed, after all.'

He strode across the cabin, and left, closing the door

behind him.

Samma's legs gave way, and she sank down on to the chair. She lifted her hand, and stared at it stupidly, as if she expected to see the mark of his lips, burning there like a brand.

He'd only kissed her hand, she told herself weakly. There was nothing in that to set her trembling, every sense, every nerve-ending tingling in some mysterious way. What would she do if—when he really kissed her? When he . . .

Her mind blanked out. She couldn't let herself think about that. She would cope with it when she had to.

And she would soon have to, a sly inner voice reminded her. 'A pleasure postponed,' he'd said.

For the first time in her life, Samma found herself cursing her own inexperience. She wished she had some real idea of what Roche Delacroix was going to expect from her—when he returned. Would he make allowances for her ignorance—or would impatience make him brutal?

She bit her lip. Oh, God, what right had anyone as sexually untutored as she was to throw herself at a man of the world like Roche Delacroix?

I can't stay here, she thought, panicking. I can't! I'll have to leave—go back on shore—find some other way out. I must have been mad.

She retrieved her espadrilles and ribbon and, picking up her bundle, went to the door. The handle turned easily enough, but the door itself didn't budge.

She twisted the handle the other way, pushing at the solid wood panels, but it made no difference. He'd locked her in, she thought wildly.

She might have come here of her own free will, but she was staying as a prisoner. And when her jailer came back—what then?

When the door eventually opened half an hour later, Samma was as taut as a bowstring.

'How dare you lock me in?' she stormed.

Roche Delacroix's expression was preoccupied, and he looked at her with faint surprise. 'I did not,' he said. 'The door sticks sometimes, that is all. I'll have it corrected when we reach Grand Cay.'

That's all? Samma thought, wincing. Because of a sticking door, and her own horrendous stupidity, she was still trapped on *Allegra* with this—this pirate.

She said. 'I've been thinking it over, and I've decided I'd prefer to forego this cruise, after all.' She picked up her bundle. 'I'd like to go ashore, please.'

'You are just hungry,' he said calmly. 'Jerome is waiting to take you to the saloon for some ham and eggs.'

The words alone made her stomach swoon, but Samma didn't relax her stance for an instant. 'I refuse to eat a mouthful of food on this boat!'

'You are such a poor sailor?' He sounded almost solicitous, but the gleam in the dark eyes told a different story. 'But we have not yet left harbour.'

'I'm a perfectly good sailor,' she said between her teeth. 'What I'm trying to convey is that I'd rather choke than eat any food of yours.'

He shrugged. 'As you please, but you will be very hungry by the time we reach our destination. Besides, I thought you would prefer to occupy yourself with breakfast while I dressed,' he added, loosening the belt of his robe. 'However, if you would rather watch me . . .'

Samma fled. Jerome was waiting outside, so there was no chance to make a dash for it, as he escorted her to the saloon.

'I'll be just within call, *ma'mselle,* if you need anything.' The words were polite, but she was being warned that he was keeping an eye on her, she thought miserably as she sank down on to the long, padded seat, and looked at the table which had been set up. There was a tantalising aroma emanating from a covered dish on a hot-plate.

She groaned silently, feeling her mouth fill with saliva. Oh, God, but she was ravenous! She'd meant every word she'd said, but surely no one would notice if she took just one—tiny piece of ham? Using her fingers, she pulled off a crisp brown morsel. It was done to a turn, of course, succulent and flavoursome, and Samma was lost.

Ten minutes later, every scrap on the platter had gone, and she was on her second cup of coffee.

'I am glad you decided to relent. I have a very sensitive chef,' a sardonic voice said from the doorway, and Roche Delacroix joined her.

The thick, black hair was slightly damp, and the sharp scent of some expensive cologne hung in the air as he came to sit beside her. He'd dressed, if that was the word, in the most disreputable pair of jeans in the history of the world. Not only were they torn, and stained with oil, but they also fitted him like a second skin, drawing attention Samma would rather not have spared to his lean hips and long legs.

She said breathlessly, 'I haven't relented at all, really. I still want to go ashore.'

He shook his head. 'That is impossible. The bargain between us is made. The next year of your life belongs to me, and it starts here on *Allegra.* You knew that when you came to me—offered yourself.'

'I—I wasn't thinking clearly,' she said huskily. She

took a deep breath. 'Monsieur Delacroix, it was terribly wrong of me to rush on board—and throw myself at you like this, and I'm deeply ashamed, believe me. But I have to tell you—it—it wouldn't work out between us—really.' She was beginning to flounder. 'I'd just be a—terrible disappointment to you—in every way.'

'Don't you mean—in bed?' She heard the grin in his voice. 'You know this from bitter experience, perhaps?'

'No.' That ridiculous blush was burning her up again!

'As I thought.' He studied her for a moment, his expression unreadable. 'So—Samantha, *ma belle*, have you made some resolve to stay a virgin all your life?'

'No—I—I mean I don't know . . .' She was stammering, and it was no wonder when his hands were on her shoulders, impelling her towards him, and every cell in her body seemed to have taken on quivering, independent life.

His eyes were darkness itself, deep obsidian wells in which she could be lost for ever. Then he kissed her, and her innocence ended. As simply as that.

It would have been easier if he'd behaved like the brute she'd feared, because she could have fought that. But he was terrifyingly gentle, awesomely persuasive, just brushing his lips across hers at first, then exploring the softly trembling contours with the tip of his tongue, coaxing her lips apart.

And when he'd achieved his objective, and gained access to the moist, inner sweetness she could not deny him, he was still unhurried, totally in control, his tongue barely flickering against hers.

His mouth pressed more insistently, became more demanding. He took her hands and placed them round his neck, pulling her against him, so that her breasts were crushed achingly against the heated muscular hardness of his bare chest.

His arms tightened round her, and his kiss deepened beyond all imagination, draining her dizzily, enforcing a submission which instinct told her was only a foreshadowing of the ultimate surrender he would ask of her.

She was breathless. She was going to faint, but if he stopped kissing her then she would die. She was burning, fevered beyond control.

With shocking suddenness he lifted his head, then put her away from him, surveying her with almost clinical detachment.

He said coolly, 'I suspect you could be a willing pupil, *ma belle*. What a pity I have neither the time, nor the patience, to be your teacher.' He reached out, and almost austerely tucked an errant strand of hair behind her ear, before straightening the straps of her dress. He said mockingly, 'Pull yourself together, *ma belle*. We have guests.'

The saloon door opened, and Clyde came in, followed by Hugo Baxter.

CHAPTER FOUR

'SAMMA?' Clyde's voice was aggressive with suspicion. 'What the hell are you doing here?'

She couldn't find her voice. Physically and emotionally, she was still reeling.

'Mademoiselle Briant is here at my invitation,' Roche Delacroix said blandly. 'She has, after all, a vested interest in our negotiations.'

Clyde stared at him. 'The hotel belongs to me, not her.'

'I was not referring to the hotel.' Roche Delacroix's eyes drifted over Hugo Baxter, inappropriately garbed for his size in Bermuda shorts and a loud tropical shirt. He gave Clyde a faint smile. 'I am sure we understand each other. Sit down, *messieurs.*' He clicked his fingers. 'Jerome,' he snapped, indicating briefly that the table should be cleared.

It was done with the speed of light. Even in those appalling jeans, Roche Delacroix was every inch the autocrat, accustomed to having his commands obeyed instantly. She couldn't understand why she hadn't recognised that when she first saw him.

'I shall be sailing soon, so there is no need for these transactions to take long,' Roche Delacroix said. 'The terms I have decided on are quite simple. Your hotel, *monsieur,* belongs to me, and I am not prepared to sell it. Instead, I shall retain you to run it for me, as my manager, and at a token salary.' He paused. 'From what I was able to see last night, some renovation is necessary. This will be carried out. I intend, you see,

49

that the hotel should make a profit. By ensuring, as manager, that it does so, you will begin to pay off the money you owe me.' He gave Clyde a long, level look. 'When the debt has been satisfied, you will be free to leave, if you wish. But not until then. And do not imagine you can cheat me. I imagine you know the attorney Philip Marquis on Alliance Street? *Eh bien*, he is to act as my agent in this matter. That is all.'

'It's not even the beginning,' Clyde said thickly, banging the table with his fist. 'I'm not acting as your unpaid servant. I can pay you off here and now, friend, and Mr Baxter here is prepared to make you a good offer for the hotel.'

Roche Delacroix shrugged. 'I am not open to offers. Monsieur Baxter's intervention is unnecessary. Nor is it certain you will be able to count on his generosity.'

'He can count on me for anything he likes,' Hugo Baxter declared, darting a look at Samma.

Roche Delacroix smiled. 'Even when I tell you that Mademoiselle Briant is coming with me?' he asked softly.

Hugo Baxter uttered an obscenity. He turned on Clyde. 'What's he talking about? You swore she'd stay here—that you'd talked her round. What the hell are you trying to pull?'

Clyde's face was grey. He stared at Samma. 'Is this—true?'

'Yes,' she said with a little sigh. There was no retreat now. Roche took her hand, and carried it swiftly and gracefully to his lips.

'You dirty little slag,' Hugo Baxter said hoarsely. 'Always too pure and high and mighty to give me a second look. But you'll go off with a man you only met last night. I always knew under that touch-me-not air you were a whore, like all the rest of them!'

The words made her cringe, but she was in no position to deny them, she thought wretchedly.

Roche said icily, 'Any more filth from your lips, *monsieur*, and you will go to be cleansed in the harbour.' His face was granite-hard as he looked at Baxter. 'Don't judge everyone by your own standards, you animal. Samantha is to be my employee, not my mistress. She is coming to Grand Cay to take charge of my young daughter.'

It was as if a bombshell had hit them, and Samma felt her own jaw dropping as well. Was he serious? she wondered dazedly. Did he really have a daughter? Until that moment, she'd had no idea he was even married. And, if he'd intended all along for her to be some kind of governess, why had he let her think—let her think . . .? She bent her head and stared at the floor, furiously aware that he was watching her, his mouth twisting in amusement.

'You can, of course, reject my offer completely,' Roche went on calmly, addressing Clyde. 'In which case, you no longer have a roof over your head, or any form of livelihood. I do not advise you to take up gambling as a profession,' he added dispassionately. 'You are neither lucky, nor always wise in your choice of opponents.' He sent a dry look towards Hugo Baxter.

Baxter began to bluster. 'What is that supposed to mean?'

'Only, *monsieur*, that if some ill wind should bring you to Grand Cay, do not trouble yourself to visit my casino. You will not be admitted.' He looked at his watch, then glanced back at Clyde. 'Your decision, *monsieur*. I have no more time to waste on you.'

There was a long fraught silence, then Clyde said heavily, 'I agree—I suppose.'

'Very wise.' Roche rose to his feet. 'I will not detain either of you any longer. Jerome is waiting to escort you off my boat. In a few days' time, Philip Marquis will call on you with the requisite papers for your signature. I advise you not to cause him any problems. *Mes adieux.*'

Allegra sailed an hour later. Samma sat slumped on the seat in the cabin, staring into space, barely aware of the powerful engine which was carrying her away to Lucifer's Cay.

'Don't you want to say farewell to Cristoforo?' Roche had come back into the saloon so noiselessly, she hadn't been conscious of his approach.

She started nervously, and swallowed. 'No. I—I never want to see it again.'

'Then you don't have to.' He walked to one of the lockers, and she heard the chink of a bottle against glass. He returned with a measure of amber liquid in a tumbler, which he handed to her. 'Drink this,' he directed briefly. 'You look as if you need it, and then I'll tell you fully what I want from you.'

She swallowed some of the cognac. It felt like fire in her throat, but it put heart into her. 'Won't your wife have something to say about you hiring a total stranger as a governess without consulting her?'

'My wife has been dead for over a year.'

Biting her lip, Samma began to say something awkwardly, and he held up a silencing hand. 'There is no need to express regret. Marie-Christine and I did not enjoy a day's happiness together, and parted immediately after the honeymoon, so don't pity me as a grieving widower. For seven years we lived completely separate lives, then she arrived unexpectedly on Grand Cay, bringing *la petite* Solange with her.'

'She wanted a reconciliation?'

His mouth curled. 'She wanted richer pickings than the maintenance payments her lawyers had exacted from me. She had not prospered during our separation. So—she moved into Belmanoir, my family home, and I occupied a suite at the casino, and life went on much as before, except that now there was Solange.'

'You hadn't seen her—had access to her?'

'I never sought it. I had put my so-called marriage behind me as a hideous mistake, best forgotten. But when I saw the child, I realised she needed a father.'

'You're very cold-blooded about it,' Samma said indignantly.

'You think so?' His brows rose consideringly. 'But then, I married Marie-Christine in an excess of hot-blooded passion, and that taught me a valuable lesson.' He paused. 'But I have tried to do my best for Solange. I have hired other companions for her, but unfortunately few of them have remained for any length of time.'

'Why not?'

He shrugged. 'For a number of reasons. Solange is not an easy child, and Belmanoir itself is remote, cut off from the social life of St Laurent, the capital.' He paused. 'And some of these ladies had a regrettable tendency to believe that—I was the one in need of companionship.'

Samma took another hurried sip of brandy.

'Unlike you, *chérie,*' he went on, mockingly. 'Who came to me only with a pistol at your head.'

She said stiltedly, 'Why didn't you tell me—what you really wanted?'

'Because you made me angry.' The dark eyes met hers implacably. 'You were so ready to believe I was

just another womaniser with an eye for a pretty
blonde. So—I decided to let you suffer a little.' He
smiled. 'And you did suffer, didn't you, *ma belle?*'

She stared at him for a long moment, then said,
'You mean that, when you told me to—undress, you
were just punishing me again?'

'The slapping I administered seemed to have had
little effect,' he said coolly. 'I thought I would try
other tactics.'

She went on looking at him. 'But you didn't know
that radio message was going to come through just
then. You couldn't have done. So—if there'd been no
message—when would the—punishment have stopped
precisely?'

'It would not have stopped.' His dark gaze touched
her mouth, lingered there in reminiscence. 'Nor
would you have wished it to,' he added almost
casually.

In the silence that followed, Samma could hear the
beating of her heart like thunder in her own ears. She
tried to think of something equally blasé to reply and
failed completely.

Roche watched her mental struggles with amusement. 'Also, *chérie,* I needed to gauge just how
desperate you were in your resolve to leave
Cristoforo. Because I must tell you now, I did not
speak the whole truth to your *beau-père* and that
other one. An employee is no longer sufficient for
my purpose. You are coming to Grand Cay as my
wife.'

There was another stunned silence. Samma said
breathlessly. 'You want me to—marry you? But I
couldn't . . .'

'I regret you have no choice in the matter,' he cut
incisively across her stumbling words. 'You are not

the only one to have reached a crisis in your affairs. Marie-Christine's parents are making a belated but sustained effort to gain the custody of Solange. Not out of affection, you understand, but because they would enjoy the allowance the court would exact on her behalf. This is not going to happen.'

'But surely they have no grounds for such a thing?'

'I am prepared to take no risks with Solange's future,' he said quietly. 'The Augustins have compiled a dossier on my shortcomings as a father for a young girl. It complains of my frequent absences from home on business, the fact that much of my income is derived from the casino, and also that Solange lacks a stable female influence in her life. All these charges have some foundation.'

'And you think if you can produce a wife—any wife, they'll just—go away?'

'No, that would be naïve. But a large part of their case would instantly cease to exist.' The dark eyes bored into hers. 'You promised me a year of your life. This is the form it will take.' His mouth curled slightly. 'To use an expression which may be familiar to you, Samantha, you have made your bed, and now you must lie on it. I do not, however, insist that you lie upon it with me.'

She said shakily, 'I don't understand any of this.'

'Next year, Solange will be old enough to go away to school, to the most respectable convent I can find for her. And then you will also be free to live your life in any way you wish—anywhere you wish. I am offering you a business arrangement, no more. You will not be a wife to me in any real sense at all, if that is the assurance you need.' He added, flatly, 'Nervous virgins are not to my taste.'

'So—we just—pretend?' The memory of that slow,

sensuous kiss was still burning a hole in her brain.

'There will naturally have to be a ceremony. Fortunately, our local laws impose no unnecessary hold-ups. If you agree, my attorney can make the necessary arrangements before we even arrive on Grand Cay.

Just like that, Samma thought, hysteria bubbling inside her. All cut and dried.

'And you think your—in-laws will be satisfied with this—charade?'

'They will not be satisfied in the least,' he said coldly. 'They are, like their daughter, selfish, greedy and deceitful. And they imagine that, knowing this, I would allow Solange to go to them? *Pauvre petite*, it is not her fault . . .'

He stopped abruptly, and she gave him a questioning look. 'What isn't her fault?'

'That my relationship with her mother was a disaster,' he said curtly, but Samma was left with the odd feeling this was not what he'd originally started to say.

'And when the year is up, you'll let me go?' She was still trying to make sense of it all. 'Isn't Solange still rather young to be sent away to school like that?'

His brows snapped together. 'I need you to play the part of my wife, *mademoiselle*, not advise me on my child's upbringing. You are, after all, scarcely more than a child yourself. When your year with us is over, you will still be young enough to train for some profession—teaching perhaps, as you once intended. Naturally, I will pay for this training, and in addition you will receive the usual alimony.' He paused. 'A new life for your old one, Samantha. Is a year really so much to ask?'

'I don't know.' Her hands twisted together. 'It's all

been such a shock. I must have time . . .'

'There is no time. Tomorrow we will arrive on Grand Cay, and I expect our marriage to take place at once.' He leaned back, studying her through half closed eyes. 'What is the matter? Are my terms not reasonable enough?' His mouth curled. 'And is it not a relief to find you have nothing to fear from my unbridled lusts, after all?'

She looked back at him coolly. 'Because Solange will be there to act as chaperon?'

'No,' he said, briefly. 'Because I have a mistress already. Is that enough for you?'

It seemed more than enough, Samma thought, swallowing the rest of her cognac. She said, 'If there's a lady in your life, why don't you get her to marry you?'

His smile was cynical now. 'Because I have no more taste for marriage than you have, *ma belle*. And my—lady might not be so ready to vanish when the year is over as you are. Does that answer you? And in return will you give your answer? Do you agree to my terms—yes, or no?'

There was a silence, then she said huskily, 'Yes, but not because I'm impressed by what you're offering. I just feel sorry for your little girl.' She put down her glass, and rose to her feet. 'And now I'd like to be alone for a while.'

'Jerome has prepared a stateroom for you.' As she began to move away, he detained her, a hand on her arm. 'May I ask if that ungainly bundle on the floor represents your total wardrobe?'

'I only brought what I could carry,' she said defensively.

'Hm.' His eyes rested with disfavour on the shabby folds of the yellow sundress. 'Then you will need clothes for your new role. Shall we call it a trousseau?'

'I'd prefer not to,' she said, with a slight catch in her voice.

'As you wish,' he said indifferently. 'However, I shall buy the clothes for you, and you will wear them. It is understood?' He tapped her cheek with a careless finger. 'Now, run away to your solitude.'

She wished she could run—preferably into the next universe, or anywhere which would take her away from him.

And this was only the beginning, she thought as she walked to the door. Ahead of her was a year—a whole year.

Oh, God, she thought. What have I promised? What have I done?

The road to Belmanoir was straight and dusty, flanked by the ripe gold of canefields. Ahead of her, Samma could see dark green forest clustering round the foot of one solitary, central peak, pointing towards the sky in admonition or warning.

But in my case, she thought wryly, the warning has come too late.

She still could not believe the events of the past forty-eight hours. She felt as if she had been caught up in some hurricane, which had left her battered, stripped of everything, including her own identity.

She gave a swift downwards glance at the slender white skirt, topped by the overblouse in a stinging shade of violet. It was not a colour she would ever have chosen for herself, but she had to grudgingly admit that it deepened her eyes to indigo. And it had been selected, like everything else in the new hide cases currently reposing in the boot of this air-conditioned limousine, by the man seated beside her in the driving seat.

Well, almost everything else, Samma thought, remembering with chagrin how he'd made her model the clothes for him. At least he'd left her in peace and privacy to choose her lingerie and swimwear.

Her eyes caught the alien golden gleam of her wedding ring, and she covered it clumsily with her other hand, biting her lip as she did so. It was less than an hour since Roche Delacroix had placed the ring on her finger, in a brief ceremony which had consisted of joint and formal legal declarations, and their signatures on a piece of paper.

Not a word, she thought, about loving or honouring. And, if that was supposed to make her feel better about the whole thing, then, in some odd way, it had been a dismal failure.

Easily made, this contract, she realised. And easily broken when its usefulness had passed.

But the ordeals of the day were not over yet. The next item on schedule was her meeting with her new stepdaughter. And this afternoon she had to face a preliminary hearing before a Judge Lefèvre of the custody battle for Solange between Roche and the Augustins. She wasn't sure which she was dreading most.

She stole a covert look at her new husband. He was wearing a beautifully cut lightweight suit in pale grey, and the black hair had been tamed to comparative respectability, but in spite of these conventional trappings he still looked as tough and uncompromising as any pirate ancestor could have done.

She wondered if he was thinking about the wedding —and that his second venture into marriage was even less promising than the first had been—but his dark face gave nothing away. He was lucky to have his driving to concentrate on, she thought, although they

hadn't encountered so much as a donkey and cart
since leaving St Laurent, the capital. Roche had been
right when he'd warned her that Belmanoir was
remote.

'You are very quiet.' His voice cut across her
thoughts, making her jump.

'I think I'm nervous.' She paused. 'Suppose Solange
doesn't like me?'

'You are being defeatist.' His brows drew together.
'Why should she not like you?'

'Because I'm the stranger you're putting in her
mother's place.'

'Marie-Christine had no place in my life,' he said
harshly. 'I thought you understood that. And it is
your task to win Solange's confidence—make her
enjoy your company. You have one great advantage
over your predecessors, after all.' His mouth twisted
in faint derision. 'You cannot simply hand in your
notice when the going gets tough.'

Samma swallowed. Lucky me, she thought.

She said quietly, 'You can enforce obedience, but
not affection. And I want Solange to be fond of
me—genuinely.'

'In a year?' The reminder was faintly brutal. 'Don't
hope for too much, Samantha.'

She bent her head. 'I don't expect very much at all.'

At dinner on *Allegra* the previous evening, she'd
tried to ask him a little about life at Belmanoir, and
Solange in particular, but his replies had been almost
terse. For a man so determined to retain the custody
of his child, he seemed to know very little about her,
she thought unhappily. For Solange's sake, she hoped
he wasn't being a dog in the manger about her.

The car turned suddenly under a high stone
gateway on to a drive flanked by tall hibiscus hedges.

Samma peered ahead of her through the windscreen, aware that her heart was beating hard and fast. She was on Lucifer's Cay, after all, and somewhere beyond the bright normality of the flowers was the house which *Le Diable* had built for himself and his dynasty.

She didn't know what she'd been expecting—a Gothic ruin, perhaps, with a skull and crossbones fluttering from the battlements. But it wasn't like that at all—just a rambling white mansion with a pillared portico, and an elegant wrought-iron balcony encircling the upper storey.

And, at the top of the steps leading to the front entrance, someone was waiting. A girl, Samma saw, no more than in her twenties, with an exquisite *café au lait* skin, and black hair coiled into a sleek chignon at the nape of her neck. The neat dark dress she was wearing did nothing to disguise ripe breasts and rounded hips, as she walked with a graceful, swaying motion down the wide, shallow flight of steps towards them.

'Roche.' Her voice was like sunwarmed honey. '*Sois le bienvenu.* It is good to have you at home again.' She turned her smile on Samma. 'And welcome to you also, *madame.*'

Samma felt something clench inside her, as Roche bent to kiss the girl lightly on both cheeks, murmuring something in his own language as he did so.

'Samantha?' He turned to her. 'Allow me to present Elvire Casson, my—housekeeper.'

His slight hesitation wasn't lost on her for a moment. Samma smiled politely, and shook hands, her mind working furiously.

'I have a mistress,' he'd said. Why hadn't he also mentioned that Samma would have to share a roof with her at Belmanoir? Or did he think she was so

young and naïve that she wouldn't think to put two
and two together and come up with the right answer?
To which the answer was—probably.

'Where is Solange?' Roche was looking around him,
frowning.

It was Elvire's turn to hesitate. 'She reacted badly to
your news,' she said at last. 'She refused to go to
school this morning, because she claimed to have a
fever. I took a pitcher of juice to her room, and she
was gone.'

His firm mouth tautened in annoyance. 'To Les
Arbres, *sans doute.*'

'*Mais oui.* Madame Duvalle telephoned to say she
was there, so I asked for her to be returned.'

Like an overdue library book, Samma thought,
bristling, as they walked up the steps into the house.

'We have arranged a small celebration to greet your
bride,' Elvire announced. 'The staff are naturally
eager to greet her.'

Samma wondered if she was merely imagining that
faintly derisive note in the older girl's voice.

She said quietly, 'I'd prefer to go straight to my
room, if you don't mind.'

'Just as you wish, *madame.* I will have Hippolyte
bring up your cases.'

Samma found herself mounting the broad sweep of
the staircase, with Roche's hand cupped round her
arm, which wasn't what she'd intended at all. He
didn't have to play the part of the devoted husband in
front of Elvire Casson, she thought, fuming. She, of
all people, would be bound to know the reality of the
situation. She wrenched herself free when they
reached the gallery, avoiding the ironic look he sent
her.

'The master suite occupies this entire wing of the

house,' he said after a pause. He pointed to a door. 'That is Solange's room.' He stopped in front of the adjoining door, and flung it open. 'And this is yours.'

It was a beautiful room. Even seething with angry resentment as she was, Samma could appreciate that. The carpet was old rose, and the walls were ivory, and these colours were repeated in the drapes which hung at the open windows, and festooned the wide Empire-style bed.

'It's—lovely,' she said stiltedly. 'Thank you.'

One wall was panelled, concealing a comprehensive range of closets, and a further door led into a small but luxuriously equipped bathroom. On the far side of the room was yet another door, and Samma pointed to it.

'What's that?'

Roche opened it, and she peered in. It was another bedroom even vaster that the one in which they now stood, its focal point being a magnificent four-poster bed standing on a dais. The canopy and coverlet were green and gold, and Samma found herself thinking, absurdly, that sleeping in that bed would be like lying in some jungle clearing, with the sun dappling through tropical leaves.

The master suite, Roche had said. And it didn't need the casual litter of masculine toiletries on the big antique dressing-chest to tell her that this was the master's bedroom.

She stepped backwards hurriedly, aware that she was flushing slightly, and that he knew it.

'Satisfied, *ma belle?*' There was open mockery in his voice.

'Not really.' Samma bit her lip. 'There doesn't seem to be a key. I'd like one—and on my side of the door, please.'

He was silent for a moment. 'That door has never been locked,' he said. 'I doubt if a key for it even exists.'

She said rather breathlessly, 'Then I'd like one made. I think our—contract entitles me to some privacy.'

'That is something we will discuss later.' He closed the door. 'Now, tidy yourself and come downstairs and meet the staff.'

'Is that—strictly necessary——?'

Roche frowned. 'Of course. In normal circumstances, a Delacroix wedding would be a major event on Grand Cay. Having cheated them of that, the least we can do is drink some champagne with them.'

'I—I'm not really in a celebratory mood.'

'Then pretend.' His smile was brief, and unamused. 'That, too, *chérie,* is part of your contract.'

She watched him stride to the door, and disappear.

She took a deep, unsteady breath as she looked around her. She supposed she should have expected a room that communicated with his, but she hadn't. Belmanoir was turning out to be full of surprises, she thought with irony. And Elvire wasn't the least of them.

She bit her lip. He probably thought a door that locked was an unnecessary refinement, because he knew how little time he'd be spending in that room. He could hardly make love to his mistress in that pagan green and gold bed with his wife within earshot, even if they all knew that the marriage existed only on paper.

She would sleep here in splendid isolation, as no doubt Marie-Christine had done before her.

She was roused from her reverie by the sound of a car approaching up the drive. She went over to the window and stepped out on to the balcony, peering cautiously over the balustrade.

The car, an elderly saloon, had stopped in front of the house, and a woman with chestnut hair climbed out of the driver's seat, and went round to the passenger side. After what could only be a low-voiced argument, the car door opened, and a child emerged, slowly and sullenly.

She was small for her age, Samma thought, and not a particularly attractive little girl, with skinny arms and legs, and dark hair scraped back into two tight and unbecoming braids. And her pugnacious scowl didn't help, either.

Samma watched the pair of them disappear into the house, and drew back with a sigh. It was clear she could expect no welcome from Solange. In fact, she was probably going to have her work cut out, but at least that would prevent her thinking about what Roche and his mistress were doing, each time her back was turned.

She flexed her shoulders wearily. Not that it was any of her business, anyway. To his credit, Roche had made no pretence about that. He had been as frank as he thought necessary about the situation.

As she walked slowly back into the bedroom, there was an impatient rap on the door, and Roche strode in.

'Why do you stay up here?' he demanded. 'Solange has returned, and the household is waiting to welcome you. Elvire has even provided a wedding cake.'

'Then let her eat it herself.' Samma found she was hovering on the edge of a dangerous combination of tears and temper.

His mouth tightened. 'What is that supposed to mean?' he asked with dangerous softness.

Samma studied the potential confrontation, and decided to back down.

'Not a thing,' she said. 'I'm rather tired, and all this pretence is a strain.'

'I have seen very little pretence as yet,' he said coldly. 'At the moment, all I recognise is the insolent brat I met on the quay at Cristoforo.'

'Then maybe you should remember I'm an artist, not an actress,' she flung back at him defiantly.

'In fact, you are my wife,' he said flatly. 'And you will not boycott our wedding reception, whatever your personal inclination.' He held out a hand to her. 'Now, come down and play your part as you agreed, and let there be no more senseless argument.'

'Very well,' Samma said angrily. 'But I don't guarantee the performance.'

He was angry, too, as he said grimly, 'Then perhaps there should be a rehearsal,' and reached for her.

This time, there was no gentleness in him at all. His mouth possessed hers harshly, and without grace. Her body was crushed mercilessly against his. She couldn't breathe. She could barely think.

Some instinct warned that to struggle, to fight, would only make things infinitely worse, so she stayed mute and passive in the punishing circle of his arms until the violent ruthless kiss came to an end at last.

She was very pale, her mouth trembling and swollen from his passion, as she looked up into his dark, relentless face.

'You—you really are a pirate, aren't you?' she managed. 'I bet the original Devil Delacroix couldn't teach you a thing.'

'Then learn not to annoy me,' he returned brusquely. 'I give you five minutes in which to join me in the *salon*.' He paused. 'And you would be wise, *mignonne,* not to make me fetch you a second time. I am sure that everyone has already drawn their own—romantic conclusions about the reason for our delayed appearance.' He flicked a deliberate glance towards the bed. 'Next time, I might justify their suspicions.'

The door slammed behind him. Samma sank down on the dressing-stool, her legs giving way under her. She stared at herself in the mirror with wide, bruised eyes.

She thought, He couldn't—he wouldn't . . . Not when he promised . . .

And paused, shivering. For what did a promise mean to a man who demonstrated quite clearly that he made his own rules?

And was, she realised, as she laid a finger on the tender, blurred contour of her mouth, prepared to enforce them.

CHAPTER FIVE

SHE had expected to find the *salon* full of people but, in fact, Roche was alone there with Solange and her companion.

Samma hesitated in the doorway, aware of the overt hostility in the child's face as her presence was registered.

'Come in, *chérie.*' Roche came swiftly to her side, drawing her forwards into the room. 'Solange, *ma petite,* here is someone I wish you to meet.'

'Papa.' The child's voice was clear, and simmering with resentment. 'Have you truly married this person?'

Samma saw his face darken, and intervened hastily. 'My name is Samantha, but usually my friends call me Samma.'

'I do not wish to be your friend,' Solange flared. 'I do not want you here. But you will not stay. The Delacroix curse will send you away, like all those other silly women.'

'Solange!' Roche's voice was like the crack of a whip. 'You will stop this nonsense at once, do you hear? And you will apologise . . .'

'I will not. It is not nonsense. She will leave. They all do.' She glared at Samma. 'Go, *madame,* while you are still safe.'

Coming from an angry little girl in broad daylight, it should have been ridiculous, yet Samma felt herself shiver involuntarily.

'You are insolent and unkind, *ma fille,*' Roche said

icily. 'If you are not prepared to welcome Samantha, then you may go to your room—and this time remain there.'

Solange looked as if she was on the verge of protest, then thought better of it, and left the *salon*, shutting the door behind her with more than a suspicion of a slam.

Samma realised she had been holding her breath, and released it slowly.

'You must excuse her, Roche.' The other woman, who had been a silent spectator until then, rose from her chair, and came forward. 'It is natural she should find her first meeting with her *belle-mère* a traumatic one.' She smiled pleasantly at Samma. 'Please make allowances for *la petite, madame.*'

'I've been a stepdaughter myself,' Samma said neutrally. 'I know what the problems are.'

'And I have been neglecting my manners,' Roche said, frowning. 'Samantha, may I present Liliane Duvalle, who is our closest neighbour?'

They shook hands. It occurred to Samma that her new acquaintance was slightly older than she'd originally thought, but she was startlingly attractive with her magnolia skin and slanting brown eyes, coupled with an entirely French air of confidence and chic.

'*La petite* is not the only one to have had a shock,' Madame Duvalle was saying with a humorous grimace. 'You kept your marriage plans a great secret, *mon ami.*'

He drawled, 'I feared the gods might become envious and steal her from me, Liliane.'

She laughed. 'A romantic notion! Allow me to welcome you to Grand Cay, *madame*—also a place of romance.'

'If that is how you regard murder, robbery and
rape,' Roche agreed levelly. He turned to Samma.
'Liliane is writing a guide to the island, *ma belle*,
which naturally includes the history of the Delacroix
family.'

Liliane Duvalle smiled. 'Which your husband
would prefer forgotten. But that is impossible, *mon
ami*. *Le Diable* and his exploits—the tourists find them
fascinating.'

'Solange seems to be equally interested,' Samma
remarked. 'Not a very savoury subject for a child of
her age, I would have thought.' She paused, then said,
trying to sound casual, 'What is this curse she
mentioned?'

Roche snorted. 'An old and foolish legend. It is said
that *Le Diable* was cursed by one of the prisoners he
held to ransom. The surprise is that it was only one of
them,' he added cynically. 'But, of course, when any
tragedy befalls the Delacroix name, it is said
immediately to be the family curse.'

'Well, Solange clearly believes in it,' Samma said,
half to herself.

Liliane Duvalle shrugged. 'Perhaps—but it is part
of her blood—her heritage. It is natural she should be
intrigued.' She smiled at Samma. 'They say, too,
Madame Delacroix, that the ghost of *Le Diable* walks
at Belmanoir.'

'Then they do not say it to me,' Roche said grimly.
'I have no patience with such idiocies.'

Liliane Duvalle heaved a sigh. 'I withdraw my
earlier statement, Roche. You are not at all romantic,
after all.' She patted his arm. 'And do not frown, *mon
vieux*. Remember, this is your honeymoon—and I am
intruding,' she added with a pretty *moue*. 'Forgive me.
I only wished to see Solange safely home.'

'We are about to have some champagne,' Roche said. 'Won't you stay and drink our health?'

'Not this time.' She smiled at Samma. 'But perhaps in a week or so, you will give me the pleasure of dining with me. In the meantime . . .' She paused.

'Yes?' Samma prompted.

Liliane looked faintly embarrassed. 'I am so fond of *la petite*. Will it be in order for me to continue my visits here? I would not wish to interfere, *naturellement.*'

'Of course.' Samma forced a smile, aware that the idea didn't fill her with total delight. It wouldn't be easy for her to form a relationship with Solange, if the child was constantly being visited by someone she preferred.

'You are too good.' She turned to Roche. 'You have married an angel, *mon ami*. Now, permit me to leave you alone together, as you must wish.'

Samma turned away hurriedly, aware of the amused irony in Roche's glance, as he escorted their visitor from the room.

When he returned, she said, 'This ghost—is this really why the others wouldn't stay?'

'Understand this, *ma belle*,' he said harshly. 'There are no ghosts at Belmanoir. Your predecessors were victims of their own hysterical imaginings, nothing more.'

'And Solange?'

'That is another matter.' He frowned. 'I dislike this preoccupation with the past. I hope you will be able to divert her thoughts into healthier channels, more suitable for her age.'

Outside in the hall, there was the muffled sound of voices, and excited laughter. Roche reached for her hand, drawing it through his arm. 'Now it begins,' he said, half to himself. He glanced down at her. 'Play your part well, *mignonne*.'

But that, Samma thought, as she pinned on an obedient smile, was easier said than done.

Judge Lefèvre was a small, rotund man with shrewd eyes behind gold-rimmed glasses.

He said briskly, 'Be seated, if you please.'

Samma sank into the chair he indicated, aware that her legs were trembling. The awkwardness of the celebration party at Belmanoir was behind her, but this promised to be the greatest ordeal so far.

She felt such a fraud, she thought passionately. Back at the house, they'd all been so welcoming, so delighted to see her, from Roxanne, the fat and smiling cook, to Hippolyte, the gardener-cum-handyman, not to mention the maids, and the casual workers employed in the house and grounds. Their delight in the fact that 'Mist' Roche' had taken a wife, and their robustly expressed good wishes had been embarrassing in the extreme—especially under Elvire's enigmatic regard.

Samma had found herself wondering if the other staff knew what had been going on between their master and his supposed housekeeper, and disapproved.

Her hands clenched together in her lap as Roche took his seat beside her, and his attorney, Maître Jean-Paul Giraud, sat down on her other side.

The lawyer was much younger than she'd expected, loose-limbed, with a smiling, attractive face. When Roche had introduced them, he had kissed her hand with an exaggerated but heart-warming admiration.

'Madame, when Roche informed me he was to be married in such haste, I admit I wondered, but now that I have seen you I understand everything. He is the most fortunate man in the world.'

As she'd walked into the judge's private office, Samma had been blushing, and she'd heard a faint hiss from the other side of the table.

The Augustins were not a prepossessing couple, both plump, with discontented expressions. Their lawyer, Maître Felix, looked irritated and resigned.

Samma hardly heard the opening statements by both attorneys. She was waiting tensely for the announcement of her marriage. When it came, she was still totally unprepared for the sensation it caused.

'*Married?*' Madame Augustin shrilled. 'What lie is this?'

'It is the truth, *madame.*' Maître Felix studied the marriage certificate, then passed it back to Judge Lefèvre. 'A valid ceremony has taken place. Your son-in-law has legally remarried.'

There was a silence, then the woman shrugged a shoulder. 'What difference does it make? Now that he has a new wife, he will simply neglect *la pauvre petite* all the more.'

'*Au contraire,*' Maître Giraud said. 'Madame Delacroix is anxious to care for Solange—to establish a stable home background for the child.'

Madame Augustin gave an incredulous laugh. 'Look at her! She is scarcely more than a child herself.'

Judge Lefèvre gave a slight cough. 'If you will permit me,' he said austerely. He studied Samma unnervingly for a long moment. 'May I ask, *madame,* if you were acquainted with your *belle-fille* before the marriage took place?'

She said huskily, 'No, I—I met her for the first time today.'

'And did it go well—this meeting?'

Samma met his gaze, and realised that he would detect any attempt at a cosy lie. She said, 'Actually, it was pretty much of a disaster.'

'You see!' exclaimed Madame Augustin, and was hushed by her lawyer.

'So,' Judge Lefèvre said slowly, 'there is little chance of any immediate rapport between you?'

'Within the near future, very little.' Samma was aware of Roche's restive, angry movement. 'But we're talking about a lifetime—the building of trust—of a stable relationship.' She took a deep breath. 'Solange, frankly, doesn't want me in her life, or anyone else for that matter, but I intend to be there for her, just the same. She may never accept me, but that's a chance I'm prepared to take. Maybe I'm too young to be a—a conventional mother to her, but I can be her friend, and that's what I'm offering, now and in the future—to be there for her when—if she wants me.' She bit her lip. 'I've been a stepdaughter myself. I don't expect instant miracles.'

'Words.' Madame Augustin dripped contempt into the thoughtful silence which followed Samma's little speech. 'We can offer *la petite* a secure, familiar home.'

'Familiar?' Jean-Paul Giraud queried. He glanced at his papers. 'I understand there was little contact between yourselves and the late Marie-Christine Delacroix.'

'My poor child.' Madame produced a handkerchief. 'Trapped in her tragic marriage to that—monster. Is it any wonder she lived like a recluse?'

Roche's face looked as if it was carved out of stone.

'Control yourself, *madame*.' The judge gave her a grim look.

'How can I?' The woman gave a hysterical laugh.
'This marriage is a trick—a fabrication by this
brute—this womaniser.' She turned the venom of her
gaze on Samma. 'You may think you have done well
for yourself, Madame Delacroix, but you will live to
regret this day, as my poor Marie-Christine did. He
used my child, and when he no longer wanted her, he
cast her aside.'

Maître Felix took her arm, trying to hush her, but
she shook him off. 'He killed my girl—he shut her in
that terrible house alone—and drove her to her death
with his cruelty and neglect. And he will do the same
with this new girl, once he has taken what he wants
from her. Wife!' She uttered a snort, then burst into
loud, dramatic sobs. 'She will soon find out what it
means to be Roche Delacroix's wife. Married to the
incarnation of *Le Diable!*'

'Babette——' Monsieur Augustin, his face sweating
and ashen, tried to calm her, as the two lawyers
exchanged discreetly appalled glances.

Above the tumult, Judge Lefèvre made himself
heard. 'There will be silence.'

Amazingly, there was. Then he spoke again slowly,
his eyes fixed meditatively on Samma. 'I am not
convinced the interests of the child Solange Delacroix
would be best served at this juncture by placing her in
the custody of her grandparents. Therefore, I shall
adjourn this matter, *sine die.*' He removed his glasses,
and inclined his head courteously. 'I wish you good
fortune, Madame Delacroix.'

And I'm going to need every scrap of it, thought
Samma as Roche's hand closed with disconcerting
firmness round her own, and he led her from the
room.

'You are very pale, *madame.*' Jean-Paul's voice was

sharp with concern. 'May I fetch you something—some coffee, perhaps?'

'Thank you.' Samma found herself in a kind of
waiting-room, furnished with easy chairs, and sank
into one of them gratefully. She accepted the coffee
Jean-Paul brought her, then looked up at Roche. 'I
don't understand. Did we win?'

'You could say so,' Roche acknowledged. 'Judge
Lefèvre has postponed any further hearing
indefinitely. The Augustins will have to think
carefully before taking any further action.'

'And they will have to find a new lawyer to
represent them.' Jean-Paul put in. '*Dieu*, but that
woman is poison!'

'The man is no better, believe me,' Roche told him
grimly. 'What do you imagine their next move will
be?'

Jean-Paul shrugged. 'To return to France. Maître
Felix intends personally to put them on the next plane
out of here.'

'I can only hope they never return,' Roche said with
disgust.

Jean-Paul smiled at Samma. 'Judge Lefèvre
preferred your honesty to their malice, *madame*. My
felicitations.'

She bit her lip. 'I wondered if I'd been a little too
honest.' She caught Roche's ironic look, and flung up
her head defiantly. 'But there have been too many lies,
too much pretence already.'

Jean-Paul kissed her hand. 'Your husband is a
fortunate man,' he told her. 'I am sorry that these
Augustins should have clouded your wedding day.'
He clapped Roche on the shoulder, with a grin. 'But
nothing will be allowed to spoil the night to follow,
eh, *mon vieux?*'

Samma swallowed the rest of her cooling coffee
with something of a gulp.

The square outside the town hall was crowded
when they emerged. Strolling pedestrians spilled on
to the road, jostling for position with cyclists and
elderly taxis brightly painted in a variety of bizarre
colours.

'Will you wait here while I fetch the car?' Roche
asked, and she nodded.

'Have I got time to do some shopping?'

He frowned slightly. 'Did we forget something
earlier?'

'No,' she said. 'It's just an idea I've had.'

She found what she was looking for in a toyshop in
a quiet side street. It was a doll with long blonde hair,
limbs that moved, and clothes which could be
removed for laundering, and almost identical to one
Samma had possessed herself at Solange's age.

Roche's brows rose sardonically when he saw her
purchase. 'I thought you did not believe in instant
miracles, *ma belle.*'

'I don't. This is—an olive branch.' She paused. 'I
suppose Solange does play with dolls?'

Roche shrugged, starting the car. 'You had better
ask Elvire.'

All hell will freeze first, she told herself silently. She
said, 'She's your daughter. Don't you know?'

'I thought I had made it clear how little time I have
been able to spend with her,' he said coldly. 'That, *ma
chère*, is why you are here, after all.'

And there was no comeback to that, she thought
despondently. In future, she would remember her
place.

And, just in case there was any danger of her
forgetting, the first person she met as she walked into

the house was Elvire, descending the stairs.

She paused in evident surprise. 'The hearing is over already?'

'*Mais oui,* and it has gone in our favour—for the time being,' Roche said.

'I am so happy for you, and for *la petite.*' She bestowed a polite smile on Samma. 'And for you too, of course, Madame Delacroix.'

Samma said with a faint snap, 'Would you mind not calling me that, please?'

Elvire's brows lifted. 'There is some other form of address you would prefer?'

Samma was tempted to say, Why don't you call me by my given name—as you do my husband? But she knew the answer to that already.

She said, 'I'll try and think of something,' and turned towards the stairs, the box containing the doll tucked under her arm.

Half-way up the flight, Roche caught up with her, gripping her arm with fingers that bruised.

He said quietly, 'You were less than polite to Elvire. May I remind you that she has been the mainstay of this household for some time.'

'There's no need.' Samma wrenched herself free. 'She's exactly the image of what a mainstay should be.'

The dark eyes narrowed. 'What does that mean?'

'Nothing at all.' Samma ran her fingers along the gleaming polish of the banister rail. 'She's—obviously very efficient,' she added lamely. She tried an awkward smile. 'I just expect—housekeepers to be older, handing out hot broth, and homespun advice. That kind of thing.'

He looked at her for a long, edged moment, then turned away with a faint shrug. 'I will see you at dinner.'

'May Solange join us?'

He glanced back, clearly surprised. 'If you can persuade her.' His tone doubted it, and Samma's spine stiffened in determination.

Solange's room was dim and shuttered, but the small mound in the bed wriggled as Samma entered.

She said cheerfully, 'I'm glad you're not asleep,' and threw back the shutters, letting the afternoon sun pour in.

The face which regarded her over the top of the sheet was still mutinous, but also distinctly woebegone.

'What do you want?' was the uncompromising question.

Samma sat down on the edge of the bed. 'To talk. To explain why we should at least try and get along together for your Papa's sake.'

'Why should we?'

Samma shrugged. 'Because men get very bored and cross when their womenfolk are always bickering,' she returned. 'You don't want Papa to get annoyed with us.'

Solange considered this for a moment. She said dubiously, 'When Maman was alive, Papa lived at the casino.'

'Well, we don't want that to happen again.'

There was a long pause, then Solange nodded slowly and reluctantly. She said, 'But I won't call you Maman.'

'I don't expect you to.' Samma kept her voice matter-of-fact, avoiding even the slightest taint of triumph. It was, after all, a very small victory. She put the doll on the bed between them. 'I brought you this.'

'Why?'

Again Samma decided nothing but the truth would do. 'As a bribe,' she said.

Solange stared at her. 'You mean—so that I will behave well?' At Samma's nod, she looked down at the doll, touching the fair hair, and the lace-edged skirts. She said, half to herself, 'I had a doll once, and when we came here, Maman said there was no room in the case.' She gave Samma a fierce look. 'But I make no promises, *madame*.'

'Nor do I—and my name is Samma.' She paused. 'Also, Roxanne tells me it's your favourite, chicken Creole, for dinner tonight.'

Solange's lower lip jutted woefully. 'Papa said I had to stay here.'

'I think you'll find Papa has changed his mind,' Samma told her gently, getting to her feet.

As she reached the door, she heard Solange say, 'But you will not stay here. When the curse begins to work on you, you will be glad to leave.'

Samma forced a smile. 'Perhaps I'm not that easily frightened,' she said lightly, and went back to her own room.

It was a delicious dinner, but it was not the easiest meal Samma had ever sat through. Solange had come downstairs, bringing her doll with her, which was a small step in the right direction.

The little girl was wearing a brown dress with a crocheted collar, which had a distinctly old-fashioned look. Roche should apply some of his acumen about women's clothing to his daughter's appearance, Samma thought. Beginning with those awful braids.

It was clear that Solange was carefully on her best behaviour. In fact, Samma thought ruefully, they were all trying rather too hard. And Elvire's presence, supervising the meal, didn't help.

If I wasn't here, Samma thought, she would probably be sitting in my place, smiling at Roche across the table, letting him refill her glass with wine.

Whereas, because of me, she's now some kind of second-class citizen. I bet she hates my guts. Because she must have hoped that Roche would marry her one day.

But there was no clue to any inner emotional turmoil in the beautiful, serene face as Elvire moved about the table.

Coffee was served in the *salon*. Samma had been too fraught earlier to fully appreciate her surroundings, but now she felt free to wander round the large room, examining the pictures—none of *Le Diable* as far as she could see—as well as the cabinets with their collections of porcelain, antique fans and *étuis*.

It was all very gracious and elegant—and founded on blood and plunder, she thought with a faint sigh as she sank down on one of the soft and massive leather sofas which flanked the hearth.

'May I have some coffee, Papa? May I?' Solange appealed, as Elvire brought in the tray, and Roche smiled faintly.

'Well, perhaps, as this is a special occasion.' His eyes met Samma's almost caressingly, and she looked away, blushing.

Life would be easier to cope with when these first, loaded days were over, and they were no longer forced to behave like conventional newly-weds, she thought uncomfortably. At the reception that morning, she'd had to stand in the circle of his arm, smiling radiantly, even lifting her face for his kiss when the toast to their happiness was drunk, and she'd felt a total hypocrite.

Roche brought her some cognac in a balloon glass. 'For enjoyment rather than medicine this time,' he told her in an undertone.

'Have you seen my doll, Papa?' Solange broke in impatiently. 'See, I can brush its hair, and it has petticoats with real lace.'

'*Très belle,*' Roche agreed gravely, sitting down beside her to admire the toy's manifold perfections.

Watching them covertly, Samma saw Solange glow perceptibly as he talked to her. He was kind, she thought, but aloof. He showed the child little open affection, and Solange seemed to accept this, not climbing on his knee, or throwing her arms around him, as anyone might have expected.

There was a soft cough, and Samma saw that Elvire had rejoined them.

'It is time Solange was in bed.' She held out a hand. 'Come, *p'tite.* I have run your bath.'

'Must I go, Papa?' Solange looked prepared to pout, then thought better of it, putting her hand into Elvire's, her doll securely tucked under her other arm.

Elvire paused. 'Will there be anything else this evening, Roche? If not, I will bid you goodnight.'

Samma stared rigidly at the floor. Who was supposed to be kidding whom? she wondered angrily.

'Thank you, Elvire. There is nothing more we require.' Roche sounded casual. '*Bonne nuit.*'

'*Bonne nuit,* Papa. Sleep well,' Solange piped, and Samma heard Elvire giggle softly as they left the room.

'Another cognac?' Roche asked.

She shook her head. She said, 'Roche—would you mind if I had Solange's hair cut?'

He burst out laughing. 'Hardly a romantic topic for our wedding night, *mignonne,* but, of course, you must do as you think best. Solange is your responsibility now.'

She said stiltedly, 'I suppose so.' She glanced at her

watch. 'I—I think I might have an early night.'

'An excellent idea, *ma belle*.' There was a note of amusement in his smooth voice, and something else—not so easily deciphered and far more disturbing. 'I was about to suggest it myself.'

Her heart began to thud, painfully and unevenly. She stole a nervous glance at him. 'Yes—well . . .' She rose, putting down her empty glass. 'If you'll—excuse me . . .'

Roche said softly, 'Not so fast.' He walked over to her, resting his hands lightly on her shoulders. The dark eyes glinted down at her. 'Are you so eager to run away from me? What refuge are you seeking, I wonder? This is, after all, my house. And you are my wife.'

She tried to pull away, but his grasp tightened. 'But I'm not your wife—not really. This isn't a proper marriage. You—you said that yourself—just an arrangement—you know you did.' She was gabbling, and she knew it.

He said, 'Ah, but that was before I was sure of you.' He lifted the hand which wore his ring. 'Now, you belong to me, *ma belle*.'

She snatched her hand away. She said breathlessly, 'You bought a year—not my whole life. Now, let me go.'

For a moment, she felt as if she was balanced on some kind of a knife-edge, then Roche released her, stepping backwards with a small, ironic bow.

She knew he was watching her as she walked to the door, and she was terrified of making a fool of herself—stumbling over her feet, perhaps, or betraying her inner strain in some other blatant way.

She didn't relax until she was in her bedroom, with the door closed behind her.

She said, aloud, 'I'm safe now.' Then repeated, 'Safe,' and wished, almost desperately, that she could believe it.

CHAPTER SIX

ALL desire for sleep seemed to have left Samma, although the bed had been turned down invitingly, she saw, and one of her new broderie anglaise night-gowns fanned out on the coverlet. And before dinner she'd found all her new clothes unpacked and neatly put away in the closets.

Elvire might only be playing at being Roche's housekeeper, as she herself was pretending to be his wife, but it was impossible to fault the way the other girl carried out her duties, Samma thought grudgingly.

She took a leisurely shower, put on her nightdress, and sat down at the dressing-table to give her hair its nightly brushing, tensing as she wondered if she could hear the sound of movement from the adjoining room.

She picked up her brush, grimacing. She would have to get used to this unaccustomed proximity, or she would end up a nervous wreck. It was his room, after all, and he was entitled to use it—or find more congenial surroundings as the mood took him, she told herself, as she began to tug the brush through her hair.

And stopped, her attention totally arrested by the noiseless opening of the communicating door.

Roche walked into the room. His hair was damp, as if he too had been in the shower, and he was wearing a dark blue silk robe, and nothing else, as far as she could gather.

She dropped her brush with a clatter. 'What are you

doing here? What do you want?'

He said quite gently, 'You are not a child or a fool, *ma belle*. I made my intentions clear downstairs.'

'But you promised you'd leave me alone—you said . . .'

'We seem to have said a great deal in our short acquaintance, and little of it makes any sense at all.' He came to her side, and lifted her bodily off the stool and into his arms in one smooth, co-ordinated movement. His voice was almost rough. 'I spent my first wedding night alone, Samantha. That is not going to happen a second time, whether you wish it or not.'

He carried her into his room without haste, and put her down beside the enormous bed. He looked at her for a long, measuring moment, then slid a finger under the narrow ribbon strap of her demure nightdress. 'Did you buy this today?'

Mutely, she nodded.

He said with a ghost of laughter in his voice, 'Then it would be a pity to tear it. Take it off, *chérie*.'

'No.' Her voice was scarcely more than a breath. 'I—I couldn't—please . . .'

'So modest?' he asked softly. 'Is it only beside swimming pools in the moonlight that you discard your inhibitions along with your clothes, my little nymph?'

'What—what do you mean?' Samma faltered, her heart doing a frantic somersault.

'I think you know.' Roche's eyes never left hers, and his thumb drew small circles on the bare flesh of her shoulder. 'Did you really think you were alone that night on Cristoforo?'

Samma gasped, colour flooding her face, as she remembered that sudden, unnerving conviction that she was being watched as she swam. 'You mean you were—spying on me?' she choked. 'Oh, you're vile . . .'

'You'd have preferred me to declare my presence—join you, perhaps?' His white teeth flashed in a wicked grin. 'I don't think so. I thought it showed considerable delicacy to remain in the background, *ma belle*, and make sure there were no other intruders.'

'You think that justifies you being a—a voyeur?' Samma pushed his caressing hand away. 'You're despicable!'

'But seeing you naked in the moonlight persuaded me to overlook your temper, my little shrew, and take you with me when I left Cristoforo.' He was openly laughing at her, she realised furiously. 'I restrained myself that night—and since—with true chivalry. But now, I want to touch—and kiss, as well as look.' His voice dropped sensuously.

'And what I want, of course, is immaterial,' Samma flung at him bitterly.

'*Au contraire,*' he said ironically. 'But I think you have needs you are not yet even aware of, my innocent wife.' His eyes moved to the hurried rise and fall of her breasts beneath their fragile cotton veiling. 'And it would be cruelty to us both to leave you in ignorance any longer,' he murmured, and held out his arms to her. 'Don't fight me any more, *mignonne.*'

His smile beckoned her, the dark gaze warm and infinitely seductive. Samma was trembling suddenly, but not only from fright. She was being besieged, she realised, by a welter of very different emotions.

She was remembering—unwillingly, vividly—the way he'd kissed her that first time on *Allegra*— wondering how it would be if he kissed her like that again . . .

With something like panic, she pulled herself
together. 'You seem to be forgetting something.' Her
voice sounded high, and very young. 'Your—your
mistress. Won't she be expecting you? She can't feel
very happy about the situation as it is . . .'

For a moment he looked almost startled, then his
expression relaxed. 'Oh, she will adapt to the change
in circumstances,' he drawled. 'In fact, she has no
choice.'

Samma felt almost sorry for Elvire, dismissed so
casually. But Roche's words reminded her just in time
that her own fate would be no different when her year
in Grand Cay was over. He would let her go as easily,
with as few regrets, she realised, wincing. But, if she
was completely his, could she just walk away when
he'd finished with her?

She said shakily, 'Well, I do have a choice, and I still
say—no. I'm not just a convenient female body for
you to—use when it suits you, then discard. I belong
to myself. And if you—if you persist in this—I shall
fight you—every step of the way,' she ended with a
little rush.

'Will you, *chérie?*' His mouth twisted. 'Eh bien, we
shall see . . .'

His hands reached for her. But before her lips had
even parted, she heard the scream in her head—high,
shrill, utterly terrified—going on and on endlessly.

Yet she wasn't making a sound, she realised, and at
the same time she saw Roche's face change from half-
amused, half-sensual anticipation to shocked concern.

'*Mon Dieu,*' he whispered. 'Solange!'

Samma was right behind him as he threw open the
child's door, and raced in.

Solange was sitting up in bed, her eyes staring, the
screams dying to small, sobbing moans when she saw

her father.

'Papa, oh, Papa! I saw *Le Diable*. He was here in this room.'

'*P'tite.*' Roche's voice was gentle, as he sat down on the bed beside her. 'That is impossible. You had a dream, that's all. A bad dream. Now, lie down . . .'

'Don't leave me.' The small hands clutched at the lapels of his robe. 'Oh, Papa, please . . .'

Samma saw him hesitate, and intervened. 'I'll stay with her—if she'll let me. After all, I'm responsible for her now.'

'No.' There was a grim weariness in Roche's voice. 'I will remain.'

He rose and fetched a chair from the corner of the room, placing it beside Solange's bed.

His eyes met Samma's. 'Go, *ma belle*,' he said with dangerous softness. 'And say a thanksgiving to whatever god you believe in, because I would not have spared you, believe me.' He added, flatly, 'There must be more of *Le Diable* in me than I thought.'

Samma stared at him wordlessly, then turned and fled back to the fragile security of her room, where she flung herself across the bed, shaking like a leaf.

Because of Solange's nightmare she had been reprieved, it seemed, at least for the time being.

And the shaming truth she had to face was that she didn't know whether to be glad—or sorry.

When Samma awoke slowly and reluctantly the next day, the sunlight was flooding into her room and, sitting in a patch of it, cross-legged on the floor, was Solange, staring at her unblinkingly.

Samma propped herself up on an elbow. 'Good morning,' she said awkwardly. 'Are—are you feeling better today?'

Solange hunched a shoulder. 'I was not ill,' she retorted. She gave Samma a speculative look. 'If you are married to Papa, why don't you sleep in his bed, in there?' She pointed to the adjoining room. 'Lisette Varray says married people sleep in the same bed, so they can cuddle and make babies.'

Samma was crossly aware of that betraying blush again. 'Well—perhaps. But last night, Papa had to look after you.'

'Not all night,' Solange denied with a shake of her head. 'When he thought I was asleep, he went away.'

'Oh.' There was a sudden hollow feeling in the pit of Samma's stomach as she registered this. So he had gone to Elvire after all, she thought. And she had no one but herself to blame, because she'd sent him there. He must have cynically decided she was not worth the fight she had promised him, and settled for what was readily available instead. She swallowed past the swift, painful lump in her throat and said, 'Do you often have bad dreams?'

Solange paused, as if weighing up the question, then she said, 'I was not dreaming. *Le Diable* was there. He came to warn you to leave Belmanoir, *madame*.'

'Oh, really?' Samma asked levelly. 'Then why didn't he come to me in person?'

Solange's expression went suddenly blank, as if this was a point of view which had not previously occurred to her.

Watching her, Samma felt an unworthy suspicion budding and coming to bloom inside her.

'What did he look like?' she asked.

Solange shrugged. 'Like a pirate,' she returned sullenly. She paused. 'And he frowned and shook his fist a lot.'

Samma stifled an unwilling grin. 'I'm not surprised. It must be very boring for him to have to tramp round this house for all these centuries, warning people about the curse.'

'It is not a joke,' Solange flared.

'I quite agree,' Samma nodded. 'And I don't suppose any of your previous companions found it very funny, either,' she added casually, looking Solange straight in the eye.

'Naturally, they were very afraid.' Solange gave a dramatic shudder. 'Who would not be?'

'Who, indeed?' Samma agreed. 'Did you have similar dreams before they left?'

Solange's gaze fell away. 'I think so.'

And I'm sure of it, Samma told herself silently. Aloud, she said, 'This is a lovely room. Did your mother like it, too?'

'She did not sleep here,' Solange said. 'She had a suite at the other end of the house. But all the rooms are pretty. Grandmère Delacroix chose all the new things in the house. She could not walk after her accident, and Papa said it gave her a new interest in life.'

Samma's brows lifted. 'What happened to your grandmother?'

'She fell off her horse,' Solange said calmly. 'It was the curse. And when Maman died, that was the curse, too.'

Samma frowned incredulously. 'Who in the world has been telling you these things?' she demanded.

Solange looked evasive. '*Tout le monde*. Everyone knows it.' She got up. 'I think I will go downstairs. Shall I tell Elvire to bring your breakfast here?'

'No, thank you,' Samma said hastily. The last person in the world she wanted to face, under the present circumstances, was Elvire, no doubt discreetly revelling in the fact that her lover still wanted her, in spite of his marriage. She tore her thoughts away from the unwelcome images beginning to form in her mind. 'Are you going to school today?'

Solange shrugged ungraciously. 'I wanted to, but Elvire said I had to stay here with you, instead.'

Samma bit her lip. Gee, thanks, Elvire, she thought. Trying to sound cheerful, she said, 'Well, you can show me over the rest of the house—and the gardens. Is there a swimming pool?'

'A big one.'

'Can you swim?'

'No.' Solange glared at her. 'And you will not make me.'

'God forbid!' Samma threw up her hands ironically. 'You don't mind if I use the pool, I hope.'

Solange shrugged again. 'It is your pool,' she returned reluctantly. 'Elvire says everything in Belmanoir belongs to you now.'

No, Samma thought with a sudden unbidden pang—not everything.

She bathed, and put on the simple dark blue *maillot* she had chosen in preference to the minimal bikinis on offer in the boutiques, topping it with a loose shift in a swirling jungle print. She collected her sketching things, and sun oil, before making her way downstairs.

She was frankly nervous about encountering Roche, or Elvire, unable to decide how she should react. But the decision was postponed, when she found no one about but one of the maids, who told her cheerfully that 'Mist' Roche' had gone into St Laurent to the casino, just like always.

Business as usual, Samma thought, and something

she would have to get used to. Roche had warned her
he spent little time at home. She stifled the troubling
twinge of regret which assailed her. After all, the last
thing in the world she wanted was Roche's
company—wasn't it?

The pool lay at the rear of the house, masked by
high, flowering hedges. To Samma's surprise,
Solange was there ahead of her, sitting on one of the
cushioned loungers, undressing her doll. Her face
intent, she made a delightful picture. Samma sat down
quietly, and opened her sketching block.

'What are you doing?' Solange demanded
eventually and suspiciously.

'Drawing your portrait.' As Solange came to her
side, Samma demonstrated. 'See, I put a line
here—and a curve here, and some shading—and, *voilà*,
we have Solange.'

'It is like me.' Solange gave an endearing hop of
excitement. 'And yet it is not. The hair is wrong,' she
added, pointing to the feathery bob and softly flicked
fringe which Samma had created.

'Not wrong, just different.' Samma touched one of
the braids. 'Have you never thought of changing your
style?'

'Maman wanted my hair like this. She said it was
suitable.'

Samma trod carefully. 'Well, I'm sure it was—then.
But you're so much more grown-up now. You can't
have pigtails for ever.'

Solange stared down at the sketch, her brows drawn
together, then jumped as a smiling voice called out,
'Bonjour.'

'It is Tante Liliane,' Solange announced, and ran to
the new arrival.

Samma's own feelings were mixed. She had agreed

to this, she told herself, but she hadn't expected Madame Duvalle to put in an appearance quite so soon. She fastened on a polite smile.

'But where is Roche?' Madame Duvalle enquired, as she sank into the chair next to Samma's, under the multi-coloured sunshade. She sent Samma an engaging smile. 'Surely he cannot be neglecting you already?'

Samma bit her lip. 'Neglecting' had too many connotations of Madame Augustin, she thought with distaste.

She said evenly, 'He has businesses to run.'

'And very successfully too,' Liliane said gushingly. 'Grand Cay is becoming quite a mecca for wealthy tourists, and Roche has been the moving force behind much of the island's development.'

'Were you born here?' Samma asked.

'*Hélas*, no. But my husband and I visited here many times. My happy memories brought me back here.' Madame Duvalle gave a faint sigh. 'It was François who inspired my interest in the island's history to begin with.'

Samma wondered whether the older woman was widowed, or simply divorced, but did not feel equal to enquiring.

'And Roche has always been so kind,' Liliane continued. 'He has rented me the former overseer's house at the plantation at a nominal sum.' She smiled. 'He may not agree with my researches, but he allows me every facility to proceed with them.'

'Is the plantation still in operation?' Samma asked, and Liliane shot her a surprised look.

'*Mais oui*, although it is run as a co-operative these days, and not controlled solely by the Delacroix family.' Her laugh tinkled. 'Has Roche not discussed the extent of his business interests with you? But how wicked, in these days of equality!'

'There hasn't really been time,' Samma said evasively.

'A whirlwind romance, *hein*? And just when one thought he would never . . .' Liliane paused, then shrugged, turning her attention to Solange, much to Samma's relief. 'You look a little pale this morning, *mon trésor.*'

'A disturbed night,' Samma put in neutrally.

Liliane compressed her lips. 'Not another nightmare—just when we hoped she had begun to forget.'

'Solange,' Samma said quietly, 'would you go up to the house and ask Elvire to bring us some coffee, *s'il te plaît?*'

Solange hesitated, then took herself off, dragging her feet.

'She is not an easy child to manage. You seem to have made a good beginning,' Liliane commented, leaning back in her chair.

'Maybe,' Samma said non-committally. She hesitated. 'If there's some cause for Solange's nightmares, it might be better if we didn't refer to it in front of her. She seems to listen to far too much round here as it is.'

'But of course you are right.' Liliane looked distressed. '*Mon Dieu*, but I am criminally thoughtless!'

'On the other hand,' Samma went on. 'If there's something I should know . . .' She paused enquiringly.

'You mean Roche has not told you—warned you? *Mais, c'est impossible, ça!*' Liliane looked aghast. 'And yet, can one blame him for wishing to bury the past?

The gossip and rumours were, after all, *formidable*.'

'Gossip?' Samma frowned.

Liliane looked at her sympathetically. 'About Marie-Christine—her death.'

'What about it?'

Liliane shrugged. 'There was an accident. Her car ran off the road, and into a ravine. She was killed instantly.'

'That's awful,' Samma said slowly. 'But why should anyone gossip about it?'

Liliane spread out her hands. 'Because it was said that the verdict was a cover-up—that Marie-Christine had in fact killed herself—crashed the car deliberately. It was known, you see, that the marriage was not a success—that they lived separately. She made emotional scenes—wild claims that the house hated her. That she would die if she had to live here alone.' She paused. 'That was when Elvire came. She was, you may know, a trained nurse, experienced in such cases.'

'No,' Samma said numbly, 'I—I didn't know.' She bit her lip. 'I still don't really understand. Was it just the house . . .?'

Liliane shook her head. 'I do not like to speak of it. I tried, you see, to be Marie-Christine's friend. In many ways I pitied her—loving Roche so much—receiving only coldness and rejection in return.' She sighed. 'It was a tragic situation. No wonder, *la pauvre,* that she turned to alcohol for consolation.'

'I—see.' Samma touched the tip of her tongue to suddenly dry lips. 'Had she been drinking when—when . . .'

'It seems so. This is when the talk began because she was not, *naturellement,* allowed the use of a car, or even to leave Belmanoir alone. Yet somehow she obtained the keys and set off. Also, no one could understand where she got her supplies of vodka. She was strictly forbidden alcohol of any kind, and Mademoiselle Casson watched her constantly. A servant, I believe, was dismissed, although nothing was proved. Yet still she continued to drink—in the end, fatally.' Liliane paused. 'The effect on the child can, of course, be imagined.'

'Of course,' Samma echoed dazedly, then straightened, as she heard the sound of voices approaching. The coffee, it seemed, was arriving.

'Elvire,' Solange pounced at the table, 'Madame has drawn this picture of me. It is good, *hein*?'

'Excellent.' Elvire arranged the coffee things with minute care, having greeted Liliane Duvalle with politeness rather than warmth. 'Madame has many talents, that is clear.' She gave Samma a bland look. 'Will Roche be returning for lunch?'

'I'm not quite sure.' Samma's hands gripped together in her lap, out of sight under the table. She thought savagely—Why didn't you ask him yourself, when he climbed out of your bed this morning?

'And that is not all.' Solange snatched up her doll. 'See, Tante Liliane?'

'But how charming.' Liliane Duvalle studied the doll with interest. 'And how clever of your *belle-mère* to find you a doll that looks like herself. You see the hair—and the colour of the eyes?'

With a sinking heart, Samma saw the animation fade from Solange's expression, as if a new and unpleasant thought had come to her.

'I—suppose,' the little girl said at last, colourlessly, and made no attempt to reclaim her toy. It was obvious that a chance resemblance, which had escaped Samma completely, had spoiled the gift for her.

And put me back at square one, Samma thought, sighing inwardly as she poured the coffee.

Liliane, aware she'd been tactless, hurried into speech. 'So you are also an artist. Do you accept commissions?'

'Not exactly,' Samma said warily.

'You should paint Elvire. She is like the portraits of the ladies in the house, only more beautiful,' Solange put in unexpectedly.

Samma felt a dismayed flush rise in her face, and saw it echoed, to her surprise, in Elvire's own heightened colour.

Elvire said sharply, 'That is nonsense, Solange,' and walked away, back to the house.

So she can actually be embarrassed, Samma thought. Amazing!

But at least she knew now how Roche and his mistress had met. She'd come to Belmanoir to act as watchdog for his alcoholic wife. Samma wondered with a pang if the *affaire* had begun while Marie-Christine was still alive, and whether the knowledge of it had driven her towards the final tragedy. The thought made her shiver.

Conversation over coffee proved desultory, and Samma wasn't sorry when Liliane Duvalle excused herself afterwards, on the grounds that she had work to do.

'My little book, which Roche hates so much,' she said with a little laugh. 'Perhaps you would care to read some time what I have completed so far—learn a little about the past of this family that has become your own.'

'Thank you,' Samma said politely. But she knew she wouldn't be taking Madame Duvalle up on her offer. I'm not a Delacroix, and I never will be, she thought. I'm just an imposter here. Another unwanted wife.

And definitely an unwanted stepmother. Samma was aware of Solange watching her, with a kind of quietly hostile speculation. And she made no attempt to touch her doll, lying half dressed and face-down beside the lounger.

She sighed inwardly. She couldn't blame Solange for being so prickly. She'd had a raw deal out of life, so far. A father who virtually ignored her, and a mother who drank. No wonder she'd lashed out at all well-meaning attempts to provide her with companionship. And, each time she'd succeeded in driving one of her companions away, it must have reinforced her doubts about her own lovableness, Samma thought with a swift ache of her heart. Whatever pranks she'd played must have been some kind of test, which no one had ever passed. Or not until now.

She longed to put her arms round Solange, and reassure her in some way, but she knew it was too soon, that they might never, in the year she'd been allowed, achieve such terms of intimacy. The person best able to help Solange was her father, she thought restlessly, but was he prepared to do it? Or was Solange, perhaps, an all too potent reminder of the wife he'd hated?

Samma shivered. Because suddenly, frighteningly, she understood only too well the desperation which must have driven Marie-Christine when she finally realised Roche would never be hers. Perhaps, to her fuddled mind, life without him would have seemed just another form of eternal darkness.

Oh, God—that's how I could feel—only too easily, she thought. And knew with a pain too deep for words that it was already too late.

CHAPTER SEVEN

SAMMA hauled herself out of the pool, and reached for a towel, blotting the water from her shoulders and arms, and wringing the excess moisture from her hair.

Her swim had refreshed her physically, but not mentally. She was still reeling from the implications of that unheralded, unwanted self-revelation.

She couldn't have fallen in love with Roche Delacroix! Common sense, logic and even decency all legislated against it. She knew so terrifyingly little about him, she thought. The only certainty was that he was quite cynically prepared to exploit her for his own purposes, and made no bones about doing so.

But as a man, and certainly as her husband, he remained an enigma.

She sighed as she walked back to the table. It was proving to be a long and disturbing day, and, as an exercise in togetherness for Solange and herself, it had to be marked down as a dismal failure. The child had barely addressed a remark to her over the delicious fruit-filled salad they had shared for lunch, or afterwards.

Now she was sitting, staring down at her portrait-sketch, her brows drawn together.

'Do you like drawing?' Samma prepared herself for another monosyllabic answer.

'I do not make very good pictures.' Solange hesitated, then pushed the sketching-block towards Samma. 'Draw Papa.'

'I already did,' Samma said wryly. 'And it wasn't a

great success.'

'Well, draw Tante Liliane.'

Well, it was something, Samma thought, as she tried to comply, but even after several attempts Madame Duvalle's likeness failed to transpire. As she scrunched up yet another page, a shadow fell across her.

Roche said, 'Employing your dubious talents, *ma belle?*'

Samma looked up with a startled, indrawn breath, aware her skin was tingling suddenly at his proximity. She said inanely, 'I—I wasn't expecting to see you.'

'*Evidemment,*' he agreed drily, his brows lifting slightly as he regarded her. 'Yet, here I am.'

'Papa!' Solange ran to him. 'Look—Madame has done a picture of me. I look very different, *hein?*'

'Very different indeed, *petite.*' Roche's face softened as he looked down at her. He tweaked one of her braids. 'Perhaps it is time we carried the difference into real life. Go up to the house, and Elvire will take you to the hairdresser in St Laurent.'

'Oh!' Solange digested this. 'And may I have my hair cut to look like this?' She held up the sketch.

He smiled. 'Take your portrait with you, *chérie,* so that you can show the *coiffeuse* exactly what you want.'

Solange needed no further bidding, her thin legs galvanised into a sprint as she made off, shouting excitedly for Elvire.

Samma pushed the sketching-block away, aware that her hands were shaking. It was just shock, she told herself defensively. She'd expected him to be away all day, and yet here he was in the early afternoon, and, judging by the fact that he was wearing only brief swimming trunks, and carrying a towel slung over one bronzed shoulder, with every intention of remaining.

She hurried into speech. 'Thank you for remembering about her hair. You—you didn't waste any time.'

He gave her a level look. 'You don't think so? Yet at times, I think I have wasted a great deal.'

She wasn't sure what he meant, but she wasn't going to hang around and find out, she thought confusedly. She said, 'Well, if Solange is going to St Laurent, I may as well go, too.'

'No.' Roche was smiling, but his tone was definite. 'I prefer, *ma femme*, that you stay here with me. I did not complete my morning's work in record time in order to spend the rest of the day alone.' His mouth twisted. 'Everyone was most co-operative when I explained I was on honeymoon.'

'But you aren't—we're not.' She took a deep breath. 'You seem to have forgotten—last night.'

'Not at all,' he said calmly. 'As you see, this time I have ensured we will not be interrupted.'

But that wasn't what she'd meant at all, she thought swallowing. She said breathlessly, 'I—I think I'll go for a swim.'

'You have been for one.' He reached out, and coiled a tendril of damp blonde hair round an exploring finger. His other hand slid down over her shoulder. 'Now, you should sunbathe a little. With me.'

As if she was in a dream, Samma watched him remove the long, padded cushions from the loungers, and arrange them deftly on the tiled floor.

Then he held out a hand to her. *'Alors, ma belle.'* He was still smiling, but there was a purpose in his face which would not be denied.

Still in that dream, Samma felt her hand taken,

herself drawn down beside him on to the softness of the cushions, while a voice in her head whispered, this can't be happening—it can't . . .

Yet it was. She lay in the circle of his arms, her body taut, the long sweep of her lashes veiling her eyes in what, it seemed, would soon be the only defence left to her. And felt, with a shock that pierced her inmost being, the first slow brush of his lips on her skin.

He was gentle, almost tender, his mouth making few demands as he explored the planes and contours of her face and throat with a slow, lingering pleasure he made no attempt to disguise.

Gradually, almost in spite of herself, Samma began to relax. The heat of the sun pouring down on them was nothing compared with the sweet, insidious warmth inside her which his caresses were engendering, as his lean, supple fingers soothed her, stroking lazily over her shoulders and back.

He drew her closer still, taking her hands and placing them on his bare chest, letting her feel through her fingertips the hard, steady beat of his heart.

He said softly, 'You think our marriage is not real, *mignonne*. Well, I am real. And—so is this . . .'

His mouth took hers with breathtaking emphasis. Samma's lips parted, half in surprise, half in involuntary response to the frank sensuality of this new invasion. Her hands stole shyly round his neck to tangle in his dark hair and hold him closer, while his own arms tightened round her in fierce reply.

That first time on *Allegra,* she thought, she'd had a hint of what passion could be. But she hadn't known even a fraction if it . . .

Roche kissed the line of her jaw, the soft pink recess of her ear, gently nibbling its lobe. His mouth

travelled downwards, tracing the column of her
throat, skimming lightly over the hollows and lines of
shoulder and collarbone to where the first soft curves
of her breasts had escaped the chaste restraint of the
maillot.

He lifted his head, a faint smile curving his mouth
as he studied the swimsuit's austere lines. His fingers
slid under the straps, propelling them off her
shoulders and down, and Samma gasped, snatching at
the slipping fabric.

'No—please.'

'Yes.' In spite of his amusement, he was inexorable.
'You are too lovely, *ma belle*, to spend our private
hours together hiding under unnecessary covering.'
He bent and touched his mouth to the sunwarmed
curve of her shoulder. 'You are like honey,' he
murmured. 'Does all of you taste as sweet, I wonder?'

'You—you mustn't . . .' She barely recognised her
own voice.

He shook his head, slowly. 'You are wrong.' His
tongue flickered sensuously across the swollen
contour of her lower lip. 'Because I must . . .'

His mouth fastened on hers in deep, insistent
demand as his hands slid down her body, sweeping
away the despised *maillot* with total determination.

Samma cried out in protest, and tried to cover
herself with her hands, but his fingers closed round
her slender wrists with almost insulting ease.

He said huskily, 'I have dreamed of seeing you like
this once more, Samantha, *ma belle*. You will not deny
me now.' He stroked her face with his free hand, then
let his forefinger glide lightly down her throat to the
valley between her bare breasts.

She had almost stopped breathing. The thud of her
pulses seemed to fill the universe as Roche began to

caress her breasts, his fingers moulding and shaping her startled flesh into delight. She felt the moist warmth of his tongue against her hardening nipples, and a little stifled cry of bewildered pleasure was torn out of her. His mouth moved on her almost fiercely in response, indulging himself in shameless pleasure, while the exploring hands feathered over her ribcage and abdomen to her hips, then down to her thighs, already involuntarily parting to receive his homage.

All her life, she thought, from some dazed and whirling corner of her mind . . . All her life, she'd been waiting for this. For the touch of those subtle, expert fingers, discovering, delighting every secret inch of her.

The last vestiges of apprehension about the sensual mystery into which she was being initiated were dissolving away, along with the remnants of her self-control.

Her body was twisting restlessly against the tormenting, arousing pressure of his fingers. She was making demands of her own now, arching towards him as she offered her breasts to his heated kisses, her total womanhood for his possession.

'Doucement, mignonne, doucement,' he muttered hoarsely. She could sense the hunger in him, like a leashed tiger, and in some strange way it added to her own excitement, her own urgency. 'I want to make it good for you.'

It was good already. Her entire body was melting, coming alive in a special way totally outside her experience or imagination, each new intimacy adding to the ferment within her.

Her need, exquisite and all-encompassing, matched his. She knew that now, in some strange way had known it from that first moment on the quay at

Cristoforo.

There were no doubts left. Even without Hugo Baxter's intervention, she would have gone with Roche, she knew. She would have been with him here and now, on any terms he offered, her senses frantic, starving for the fulfilment he was offering.

He lifted himself away from her slightly to strip off his trunks. He was trembling now, his own restraint at breaking point.

Last night—a lifetime ago—Samma would have been too shy to look at him. Now she stared without guile, filling her eyes with the sheer magnificence of his body.

But as he came down to her, drawing her back into his arms, she tensed suddenly, an odd frisson lifting the hair on the back of her neck.

'*Qu'est-ce que tu as?*' Immediately he sensed the change in her, the withdrawal.

She said breathlessly, 'Someone's watching us.'

'No, *ma belle.*' His lips soothed hers. 'We are quite alone, I promise. Now come to me . . .'

'*No.*' She tried to push him away, looking round desperately for something with which to cover herself. 'There is someone. I knew it that night at the hotel when you watched me—and I know it now . . .'

He said tautly, 'Are you trying to punish me for that? Be still, *chérie.* I need you so much. Let me show you—let me love you . . .'

'I can't!' Samma shook her head in violent negation. 'Not with—someone there. It must be the gardener . . .'

'I gave orders we were not to be disturbed. Neither Hippolyte nor anyone else would dare to intrude. I tell you, there's no one . . .'

'But there is.' She pounded on the cushion with her clenched fist. 'Someone revolting—watching us.'

Roche said something under his breath, then reached for his towel, knotting it round his hips.

Samma watched him stride round the pool, pausing every now and then to examine the tall shrubs which gave the area its privacy. But she knew he wouldn't find anyone. The tension had relaxed suddenly. Whatever presence had been there had now gone.

By the time he returned, Samma had dragged on her *maillot* and covered it with her shift, and was sitting nervously, her arms clasping her knees to her chin.

His anger as he looked down at her was almost tangible.

'No one,' he shot at her. 'As I predicted. Or was it just a ploy to keep me at arm's length yet again, my reluctant bride?'

She shrank. 'You—know it wasn't.'

'Do I?' His voice was harsh with cynicism. 'Perhaps you thought it would be amusing, *ma chère,* to make me suffer a little for a change. To get your own back for having been—forced into this marriage. If so, your plan has been singularly effective. *Dieu,*' he added bitingly, 'I haven't ached like this since adolescence! Next time I attempt to distress you with my attentions, why not simply use your knee? It has much the same effect.'

Samma shook her head, unable to speak because sudden tears were choking her throat, and stinging her eyes.

'Oh, spare me that,' he tossed at her contemptuously. 'I thought I had made it clear I am not impressed by weeping, or hysterics. Or by an overwrought imagination,' he added crushingly.

Samma straightened, her face flushing, 'First you imply I'm lying. Now you insinuate I'm seeing things. Well, I'm not. I don't believe in ghosts—or

Le Diable. And I won't be driven away by these stories—or frightened to death, either.'

He squatted beside her, taking her chin in a bruising grip, making her face him. 'What do you mean?'

She couldn't draw back now, so she said, 'Marie-Christine—why didn't you tell me about—the way she died?'

'Because I hoped it would not be necessary for you to know,' he said grimly. 'Clearly, someone has wasted no time.'

'You can't expect to keep something like that quiet.'

'Perhaps.' He sighed harshly. 'It was a bad time in my life. I did not want it revived, even in the telling.'

'But hadn't I a right to know—to be told—for Solange's sake, if nothing else? It—it must have been a terrible experience for her.'

'Is that really your concern?' Roche's mouth was hard. 'Or are you asking yourself, as so many did, not least *la famille* Augustin, whether my violent ancestry suddenly reasserted itself and I supplied the means to rid myself of Marie-Christine?'

'No.' Samma shook her head violently. 'No, that never occurred to me.'

He released her almost contemptuously. 'I wonder if I believe you.' He shrugged. 'Make no mistake, *ma chère.* I hated Marie-Christine enough to kill her with my own hands. But I hated the bitch she'd been, not the pathetic wreck of a woman who came to Grand Cay.' He paused. 'She was drinking herself to death, Samantha. There was no need for me to hasten the process.'

She shivered. 'That's—horrible.'

'It was a glimpse of hell,' he said. 'Her death—the inquiries which followed—the rumours and suspicion.

I felt dirty. And guilty, too.' His mouth twisted. 'Almost the guilt of a murderer, although my hands were clean. The week before her death, she had been phoning me each day, begging me to let her leave Belmanoir, and move to a hotel in St Laurent. She was irrational, incoherent, and I wouldn't listen to her. She had appeared at the casino a few times during her early months on Grand Cay—made scenes—been ill. I could not face that again. I did not realise her rantings were a cry for help that I could not give.' He sighed. 'She phoned me that last night, but I was busy and I refused to take the call. Somehow, she obtained the keys of Elvire's car and set out—presumably to find me. But she never reached St Laurent.' He gave her a hard look. 'So, now you know.'

'But why did she want to leave Belmanoir so badly?'

He rose to his feet. 'I thought you had already guessed, *chérie.*' His tone flicked at her like a whip. 'She was frightened—scared of the Delacroix curse. What else?'

He turned and walked away, leaving Samma, white-faced and shaking, staring after him.

For a time, Samma stayed where she was, her mind in total turmoil, looking blindly into space; then she got to her feet, and made her way stumblingly back to the house.

She went upstairs, and along the gallery to their suite, where she knocked on Roche's door. There was no answer, but she could hear the distant sound of running water, so she opened the door and walked in. As she'd expected, the room was empty, but the bathroom door was ajar, and it was clear Roche was using the shower.

Samma lifted a hand and pushed her sweat-dampened hair back from her face with a small, weary gesture. She was still trembling, and her awakened body ached for fulfilment. The temptation to strip off what she was wearing and join him under that cool rush of water was almost overwhelming, but she resisted it.

She had to keep her mind clear. She must say what she had to say before her courage deserted her.

It seemed a long time before he came back into the room. He was already half dressed, sliding his arms into the sleeves of a shirt, and he checked abruptly when he saw her, his brows snapping together.

She hurried into speech. 'Roche—we must talk . . .'

'I thought we just had,' he said curtly. 'I regret I do not share your apparent fascination with the supernatural.'

Samma bit her lip. 'I don't believe in that, either,' she said, her voice quivering slightly. 'There was someone watching us. I swear there was.'

He gave her a sceptical look, and began to tuck his shirt into the band of his cream trousers.

'Is that what you came to say?'

'No.' In the folds of her shift, Samma's hands clenched into nervous fists. 'There are some things—about Marie-Christine—which don't make any sense.'

'Now there we are in agreement.' Roche picked up a tie, and began to knot it round his neck. 'Which things in particular?'

Down by the pool—all the way back to the house, she'd been thinking over what she'd been told, adding up the facts and reaching some disturbing totals.

Dry-mouthed, she said slowly, 'Elvire was supposed to be looking after her, wasn't she? Yet Marie-Christine was drunk again—and the keys of the car were—there for her.'

There was a silence, then he said too quietly, 'What are you trying to say? Be very careful, *ma belle*.'

She tried again. 'Was Elvire—a stranger to you when she came here?'

'No.' Still that soft, dangerous voice. 'I had—known her for some time. But she had been away from Grand Cay to train as a nurse. Didn't your—informant tell you that?'

'Yes.' Samma swallowed, aware she was in deep water and out of her depth. 'As a nurse, shouldn't she have kept a closer eye on her patient—guarded against that kind of thing?'

'She was also trying to look after Solange,' he said curtly. 'She had searched Marie-Christine's usual hiding places for bottles, and found nothing, and the car keys were a spare set. She was putting the child to bed when Marie-Christine left the house.' His eyes narrowed. 'What exactly are you implying, *ma chère?*'

She spread her hands desperately, 'Roche, I know you care for her—I'm not a fool—but hasn't it ever occurred to you that your relationship might have made her feel possessive about Belmanoir—resentful of Marie-Christine?'

'You don't know what you are talking about,' he said harshly. 'It is because of our relationship that I would trust Elvire with my life.'

And with Marie-Christine's? she thought, but did not dare utter it aloud. Instead she said, 'If she's a trained nurse, isn't she rather wasted here as a house-keeper? Isn't it time she was getting back to her career?'

'I think that is a decision she must make.' He picked up his jacket. 'Now, if you will excuse me . . .'

She said in a little rush, 'And if I say I'd prefer her to leave—what then?'

Roche's face darkened. He said with icy emphasis, 'Elvire stays here for as long as she wishes. May I remind you, Samantha, this was her home before it was yours. I owe her a roof over her head, and more.'

'Even if it's my roof?' She took a deep breath. 'Roche, I—I don't want her here any more . . .'

He said flatly, 'That is unfortunate,' and walked past her to the door. He glanced back. 'But it is not your choice.'

She said huskily, 'But I can choose, and I do. If Elvire stays here, I—I won't let you touch me again.'

There was a loaded silence, then he shrugged. 'Then that is your decision, *ma femme*. However, I promise your nights will be lonelier than mine,' he added with cynical mockery, ignoring her little wounded gasp. He paused. 'When Elvire returns, you may tell her I shall not be here for dinner this evening. She is still our housekeeper, and the domestic arrangements are her concern, so be civil, if you please.'

Samma looked at him, misery clenching inside her like a fist. Now, it seemed, it had been her turn to gamble—and lose. She realised how Clyde must have felt.

'Very well.' She moistened her lips with the tip of her tongue. 'Will—will you be back later?'

'At bedtime, you mean?' he asked derisively. 'Perhaps, *madame*. But, under the circumstances, why should you care?' He gave her a mirthless smile and pointed to the communicating door. 'Your room is there,' he added curtly, and left her.

CHAPTER EIGHT

BY THE time Samma got downstairs, Roche was
already leaving, his car disappearing down the drive
in a faint cloud of dust.

She didn't even know why she'd followed him—
what she could have said even if she'd managed to
detain him. But she was too late, anyway.

She wanted, she found, quite desperately to cry, and
turned back into the silent house, seeking the refuge
of the *salon*.

Lying across one of its sofas, she gave way to all the
emotional confusion and uncertainty of the past few
days, letting it wash out of her in a storm of weeping
which left her drained but calm, once its force had
been spent.

She had not, she realised at last, been crying wholly
for herself, but for the look of bleak and lonely bitterness she had seen on Roche's face as he'd turned away
from her.

Just for a moment, she'd seen a crack in the tough,
self-assured, dominating façade he presented to the
world. For an instant, he'd been vulnerable, and if
she'd pulled herself together in time there might have
been something she could have done to draw them
together, not just physically, but in some deeper,
more important way.

But who was she trying to fool? she thought, as she
sat up, pushing the hair back from her tear-wet face.
Elvire was there ahead of her, so deeply entrenched in
his heart and life, it seemed, that there was no room

for anyone else.

She'd been a fool to attack Elvire directly, she castigated herself with bitterness. She should have realised that Roche would defend his mistress and believe no wrong of her, no matter what the evidence might be against her. Yet there was no real evidence—except that Marie-Christine had clearly had access to alcohol, and a set of car keys which should not have been lying around—and certainly no proof.

She remembered Liliane Duvalle's half-embarrassed remarks about scandal and rumour. Was it any wonder? she asked herself with a sigh.

But if there had been any real case against Elvire, even if it was only negligence, wouldn't the authorities have taken some action? Or would they have hesitated to cause even greater offence to the wealthy and powerful Delacroix name, and settled thankfully for a verdict of accidental death?

Samma thought about Elvire, and her serene beauty. Was she really capable of fuelling Marie-Christine's drinking problem, then encouraging her to drive to St Laurent?

Or was she just inventing a case against Elvire, because they were rivals?

Except that it was no contest, she reminded herself painfully. Roche had shown her plainly where his loyalties, and whatever love he was capable of, truly lay.

That afternoon, he'd decided to satisfy the transient desire that he could have felt for any nubile girl who'd crossed his path, and Samma knew she ought to hate and despise herself for surrendering so readily to his passion, when she knew he didn't really care about her.

And if she *had* given herself to him, what kind of

life could she have expected afterwards? Would she
have had to share him with Elvire—establish some
kind of *ménage à trois?* Roche with his harem, she
thought, shuddering. Even the thought of it made her
feel physically sick.

Yet she couldn't escape the fact that she loved him,
and wanted him more than she'd ever wanted
anything in her life.

But, if she was to keep her sanity and her self-
respect, she had to remain aloof, she thought drearily.

As she got to her feet, she caught a glimpse of
herself in the big mirror above the empty fireplace,
and grimaced. With her tear-stained face and swollen
eyes, she looked barely older than Solange herself.

She would have to wash this evidence of her
wretchedness away, she thought. They would be back
soon, and she didn't want Elvire to have the
satisfaction of seeing she'd been crying.

She went upstairs, letting the silence of Belmanoir
enfold her. For a place with such a chequered history,
it had an extraordinarily peaceful atmosphere, she
thought, as she went along to her room, and across it
to the bathroom beyond. She pushed open the bathroom door, then stopped with a little cry.

Scrawled crudely in lipstick—her lipstick—across
the mirror above the vanity unit was the message,
'You are cursed. Go now.'

Oh, really? Samma thought wrathfully, picking up
the ruins of her lipstick and examining it. I think it's
time I did some cursing on my own account.

The fact that only the bottom section of the mirror
had been used, and that there was a certain awkwardness about some of the lettering, pointed the finger, as
she'd already suspected, directly at Solange.

Her previous companions must have been a pretty

poor lot if they'd let themselves be chased away by something as rudimentary and obvious as this, she thought, looking at the mess with disfavour. But perhaps this was just for starters. Well, it could end there, too!

She washed her face and hands, brushed her hair, and was on her way downstairs again when she heard the sound of a car drawing up outside. For a moment, her heart leapt, as she hoped, desperately, that it might be Roche.

Then she heard Solange's excited voice, and realised her mistake.

The child flew into the hall as Samma reached the bottom of the stairs. 'Look at me!' she called out triumphantly.

'I am,' Samma assured her. She could hardly believe the difference the new hairstyle had made, and not just to Solange's physical appearance. She seemed altogether more confident, almost incandescent with happiness.

'Where is Papa?' she was demanding imperiously. 'I want to show him how I look.'

Samma bit her lip. 'Actually, he's not here right now. He had to go back to St Laurent for an important meeting,' she improvised hastily, only too aware of Elvire, a silent audience in the doorway.

'Not here?' The delight faded from Solange's face, as if a lamp had been switched off inside her. 'But why has he gone? Why couldn't he wait to see me?'

'He'll be back later,' Samma said, mentally crossing her fingers. 'You can put on your prettiest dress, and dazzle him then.'

Solange's scowl was fixed on her with the force of a laser beam.

'I have no pretty dresses, and I don't believe Papa

has a meeting at all. I think you quarrelled with him,
like Maman, and now he has gone away again.'

Samma felt a hint of betraying colour rise in her
face, but she kept her voice level. 'You are being rude,
Solange.'

'Then send me to my room. Isn't that what usually
happens?'

'I suppose so,' Samma acknowledged drily. 'But
this time I'm going to send you to *my* room. My
bathroom to be exact.' She turned to Elvire. 'Please
would you ask one of the maids to take Solange some
cleaning stuff. She's had an accident with my lipstick,
and I think she should be the one to clear it up.'

There was a long silence, and Solange stared down
at the tiled floor, her face crimson. 'I don't know what
you mean,' she said sullenly, at last.

'I think you do,' Samma said quietly. 'And please
don't play any more tricks like that, because they
won't work. I'm here, and I mean to stay.'

And Elvire, who was listening to the interchange
with obvious astonishment, could take that last
remark to heart as well, she thought.

Solange, reduced to a guilty silence, trailed
reluctantly upstairs. When she had gone, Elvire said
quietly, 'You must excuse her, *madame*. She gets so
little of Roche's attention, and yet it means the whole
world to her.'

And to me, Samma thought desolately. And to you.

Aloud, she said, 'You really don't have to tell me
that.'

'No.' Elvire's tone was curiously dry. She paused.
'Will Roche, in fact, be home for dinner?'

Samma shook her head with an effort. Even that
much of an admission was torture, she thought,
making herself meet Elvire's gaze. But there was none

of the thinly veiled triumph she'd expected. Instead Samma saw bewilderment, and something which could almost have been compassion, before Elvire shrugged and turned away. 'Then I will warn Roxanne.'

Samma wanted to ask, Did you leave Solange at the hairdressers' and come back here? Were you hiding down at the pool, watching us?

But her own common sense told her it just wasn't possible. Perhaps Roche was right, she thought, with a sigh. Perhaps all this talk of pirates and curses was making her imagination run away with her.

The bathroom mirror was restored to its usual pristine state, but Solange refused point-blank to come down to dinner, so Samma ate a solitary meal in the big dining-room, forcing the food down her taut throat.

She was sorely tempted to sacrifice her pride, and follow Roche to St Laurent, but what if he wasn't at the casino at all? And, anyway, what could she possibly say or do to bridge the gulf yawning between them?

I could try the truth, she thought, biting her lip. I could tell him I love him.

But he might not believe her. Or, even worse, he might be embarrassed or irritated by such a declaration from her. And she couldn't risk that.

At the same time, she wasn't prepared to sit passively by, and concede victory to Elvire.

So she would offer him what she knew he wanted—her body.

She spent a long and restless evening, trying to figure out how to approach him. She could try flinging herself into his arms, she thought, but they might not be open to receive her, after the way she and Roche had parted earlier. Or she could be matter-of-fact, and tell him she hadn't meant what she had said, and wait for him to make the next move. Except that he might thank her politely, and walk away again.

Eventually, just after midnight, she decided what she would do.

She went up to her room, bathed and scented herself, and brushed her hair over her shoulders until it shone. Then she went on bare and silent feet across her room, into his, and stood for a long moment, looking at the empty, moonlit bed.

Trembling a little, she slipped off her nightgown and dropped it beside the bed, where he would be bound to see it.

Then she slid under the covers, and lay there waiting.

It was a long time later, and she was almost asleep when the sound of the car jolted her back to awareness.

She tensed, imagining him entering the house, making his way up the stairs, and along the gallery to his door. By the time the door actually opened, she was as taut as a bowstring. She closed her eyes, willing herself to relax, her every sense conscious of his tall figure standing there in the shadows, watching her. Unmoving.

Perhaps she should sit up, she thought confusedly. Hold out her arms to him. Say his name.

And then she heard it. The slight click of the door as it closed again—behind him.

Propped up on one elbow, Samma stared incredulously into the darkness, and realised she was alone.

It was what she had dreaded. She had offered herself. And Roche had rejected her.

*   *   *

Samma replaced the cap on her suntan oil and
screwed it meticulously into place before putting the
bottle back on the table. She was strongly tempted to
throw it as far as the horizon, swearing loudly as she
did so, but she resisted the impulse. After all, the
suntan oil was blameless.

I've got to find something to do, she told herself.
Something to stop myself from thinking.

Three endless days had limped past since the night
of her humiliation in Roche's room. Days which she'd
spent in more or less solitary splendour beside the
pool. And her nights had been spent alone too. She
had fled back to her own room after Roche had left
her, too stunned even to weep, and lain awake in the
darkness, asking herself over and over again what else
she could have expected.

The following day, a surprised Hippolyte had
arrived at the suite to fix to the communicating door
the lock she had once demanded.

And that, Samma thought wretchedly, had been
that.

Solange had returned to school, and came back in
the early afternoon. She'd been obviously nonplussed
by Samma's cool reception of the warning message,
and there'd been no signs or portents since, Samma
thought drily. But there hadn't been much contact
between them either, and this she regretted. Solange
had retreated into a silent hostility which Samma
found difficult to breach.

About the only time she made a voluntary remark of
any kind was at dinner, when her father was present,
Samma realised, sighing. But, as Roche did not come
home every evening, mealtimes were generally quiet
affairs.

And Roche himself? She swallowed painfully. He

treated her with a cool politeness which somehow hurt more than if he'd followed his daughter's example, and totally ignored her.

The only time he'd looked at her as if she was a human being had been the previous evening, she thought miserably, and then only because they'd almost had a row.

Samma had sought him out as he was preparing to drive back into St Laurent to the casino.

'Could I speak to you, please?' Her voice was awkward. She felt as if she was being interviewed by some head teacher, or potential boss. But then, of course, that was what Roche really was—her employer, as she should have made herself remember, instead of indulging herself with crazy fantasies about love and passion. Impossible now to think this cold-eyed stranger had held her naked in his arms and woken her senses to vibrant life.

'Can it wait?' Roche glanced at his watch. 'I am in a hurry . . .'

'I just wanted to ask if there was anything I could do—any kind of job at the casino.' She saw his brows snap together, and hastened on. 'I—I do seem to have rather a lot of time on my hands, and I wondered . . .'

'Are you planning to recreate your role as hostess, perhaps?' he asked derisively. He shook his head. 'I think not.'

Samma flushed hotly. 'I wasn't thinking of that. But if there's nothing at the casino, perhaps I could use my drawing in some way . . .'

'Your career as a pavement artist is also at an end,' Roche said grimly. 'May I remind you that you were warned the house was isolated, and that you are here to befriend Solange.'

'Oh, sure,' Samma said bitterly. 'And you can see

what an enormous success that is! I'm wasting my time here. She doesn't want me. In fact, she doesn't want anyone but you. If I went away, she wouldn't even notice.' She bit her lip. 'Really, that could be the best solution all round. If I just left . . .'

'You will do nothing of the kind,' he said icily. 'I said a year, and I meant it. Attempt to break our agreement, and you will be sorry, Samantha. I promise you that.'

She said in a low voice, 'I'm already sorry,' but he'd left, and didn't hear.

Now, the following day, Samma found herself wincing away from the memory of it. There was no need for him to be so dismissive, she thought sadly. She'd no intention of peddling her portrait sketches in public again. From what she'd been able to gather, it seemed art teaching was minimal at Solange's school, and she'd considered volunteering her services, as a temporary tutor.

I can't spend the whole year swimming, sunbathing and being ignored, she told herself. She could feel a kind of sympathy for Marie-Christine, and wondered, not for the first time, what could have happened to make the marriage go so disastrously wrong.

Roche had claimed, she remembered, to have spent his first wedding night alone, so it seemed their relationship had been in crisis from the first. And yet there was Solange . . .

Perhaps he'd been in love with Elvire all along, and had only married Marie-Christine on the rebound. In that case, why hadn't he proposed to Elvire the second time around?

Perhaps because he knew such a marriage would stir up again all the gossip and speculation about

Marie-Christine's accident, and give the Augustins an additional weapon in the battle over Solange.

She shivered. Well, that battle was over at least, but she was the one left wounded.

Oh, come on, she adjured herself impatiently. Stop pitying yourself! Roche brought you here to do a job, not become emotionally involved with him. You have no one to blame but yourself.

She walked to the edge of the pool and dived into the water, covering two lengths in a swift, racing crawl.

As she hauled herself on to the edge, she saw to her surprise that Solange had arrived. It was the first time the child had been down to the pool area since Samma had sketched her. And, although she was looking thoughtful, she wasn't actually scowling for once.

Easy, Samma warned herself wryly, as she smiled at her. *'Bonjour,* Solange. *Comment ça va?'*

The thin shoulders moved in a slight shrug. She looked past Samma to the sunlit dance of the water. 'Is it hard—to swim?'

Samma swallowed her surprise. 'Why—no! I thought you weren't interested in learning. Would—would you like me to teach you?'

There was a pause, and Samma felt that the child was nerving herself to answer. But why? she wondered. Most children of her age, with a private swimming pool of this size, would be able to swim like fishes already.

'Yes, *madame.* I would like to learn.'

She's actually asked me for something, Samma thought in amazement. Is this some kind of break-through?

She said with deliberate casualness. 'Well, fine. Shall we make a date for the same time tomorrow—

when you come back from school?'

'Could it not be now?'

'Of course, if you want.' Samma hid her jubilation.
'What about a costume?'

'I have one.' Solange's voice sounded oddly
strained, as she tugged a dark green swimsuit out of
her school bag. Clearly, she'd come prepared and
meant business.

When she had changed, Samma took her to the edge
of the pool, and sat beside her, encouraging her to
dangle her legs in the water. Solange sat and listened
obediently, but her skin had a distinct pallor, and she
looked more uneasy by the minute.

Samma went into the water, and demonstrated some
leg movements.

'That's all you have to do,' she said. 'I'll hold you
up by your arms and shoulders. You don't even have
to get your face wet, if you don't want to.' Some
people she knew had what amounted to a phobia
about such things, and maybe Solange was one of
them.

She held out her hand to the child. 'Come on,' she
said. 'Trust me.'

For a moment she thought Solange was going to
back away, then slowly, gingerly, the child allowed
herself to be tugged gently into the water, her hands
clinging to Samma's. She looked very small, and very
sallow, as if the action was taking every ounce of
courage she possessed.

Yet this is the shallow end, Samma thought,
puzzled, and I've promised I won't let go of her. What
is it, I wonder? At the hotel, after all, quite tiny tots
had hurled themselves gleefully into the pool.

Perhaps I should have waited, Samma thought.
Bought her some of those armbands, or a ring.

She gave Solange a warm smile. 'That's fine. That's great. Now, I'll support you—like this, and you lie on top of the water, and kick like I showed you.'

Solange closed her eyes, gritted her teeth, and kicked out in entirely the opposite direction. Her foot landed squarely and painfully in Samma's midriff, and she doubled up instinctively, gasping. Solange kicked out again, this time at her legs, catching Samma off balance, and they both went down under the water in a welter of arms and legs and spray.

Choking, Samma struggled up, in spite of Solange, who was clinging like a limpet, still kicking her, and punching and scratching at her arms and shoulders, all the time screaming in a thin, reedy voice.

Shocked though she was, Samma thought, 'This isn't just panic. This is something else . . .'

She hoisted the struggling child out of the water with an immense effort, and crawled after her.

Trying to catch her breath, she began, 'Now what in the world . . .?'

Then she heard Solange scream, 'Papa—Papa! She made me go in the water. She tried to drown me! Oh, Papa!'

'*Qu'est-ce qui se passe?*'

Eyes stinging, and still spluttering from her unexpected ducking, Samma saw Roche striding towards the pool edge, his face dark with fury.

Solange ran to him, still crying out pitifully. 'Papa, she dragged me under the water. I nearly drowned! I told her I did not want to swim—ever, but she made me. She hates me—she hates me.'

Roche turned on Samma. 'Is this true? Did you make her go in the water?'

'She pulled me in,' Solange put in tearfully. 'I did not want to. I told her that when she came here. I told her she could not make me.'

Samma scooped her hair back from her face, thinking furiously. She said, trying to keep her voice level, 'Yes, that's right—but today I had the impression that she'd changed her mind.'

'She seized hold of my hands. She would not let go of me. She pulled me off the edge,' Solange chimed in again. She lifted her fists and scrubbed at her wet eyes, but not before Samma had glimpsed an unmistakable gleam of triumph.

'You treated a nervous child like that?' Roche asked incredulously. He stroked his daughter's wet hair. '*Tais toi, chérie.* It is all over now.'

Elvire came flying down the path. 'What is it?' she demanded. 'I thought I heard screaming.'

'You did,' Roche confirmed grimly. 'My wife decided to give Solange an unwanted swimming lesson.'

'Ah, *mon Dieu!*' Elvire put her hands to her mouth in unsimulated horror.

Samma said huskily, 'Now, wait a minute. I don't know what's going on here, but there is another side to all this. Solange asked me to take her in the pool.'

Roche shook his head. 'You misunderstood,' he said curtly. 'She would never do such a thing.' He turned to the still weeping Solange, now muffled in a towel. 'Go to the house with Elvire, *ma petite.* You are safe now.'

Samma was gasping as Solange was led away. 'Safe?' she echoed angrily. 'What's that supposed to mean? You think I would have let her come to any real harm?'

'You have already done her immense psychological damage,' Roche returned furiously. 'You admit she told you she did not want to swim, and yet you forced her.'

'I did nothing of the kind.' Samma paused, remembering. 'Well, she did seem a bit reluctant when it came to it, but there was nothing—nothing to prompt all this fuss. I got her into the water, and suddenly she went mad.'

'I am not surprised,' Roche said, his mouth tightening. 'It must have been another nightmare for her.'

'But swimming's a perfectly normal, healthy activity,' Samma protested. 'I was delighted when she seemed to show an interest. I thought I might be getting somewhere at last.'

'And so you allowed that to outweigh your judgement when you saw her fear?' His brows drew together. 'I thought better of you than that, Samantha.'

She said wearily, 'I seem to have been found guilty of a crime I didn't know existed. Will you please explain why it's so impossible that I should be telling the truth? Why shouldn't Solange have changed her mind about learning to swim?'

He said quietly, 'Because you, *ma chère,* are not the first person to try to teach her. Marie-Christine also made an attempt. She threw Solange in—at the deep end—and followed her. But—she was drunk, as usual, and did not realise that Solange had sunk like a stone. If Elvire had not arrived just in time, there would have been a terrible tragedy. Now do you see why there must have been a misunderstanding today? Since her ordeal, Solange has never willingly gone near the water again. For months, even a simple bath at the end of the day terrified her.'

'Oh, God!' Samma's mouth was dry. 'Oh, God—why didn't you tell me about this—warn me?'

'Because it should not have been necessary,' he said shortly. 'Solange has kept her distance from the water's edge ever since. It never occurred to me you would be cruel enough to ignore her obvious fears. I had forgotten, of course, how insensitive and impetuous the young can be.'

'Is that what you think?' Samma shivered, feeling suddenly sick. Solange had set her up, of course. That whole scene had been deliberately staged because the child knew Roche had returned home unexpectedly, and would be coming down to the pool. This was Solange's revenge, she thought, for the humiliation of having to clean the lipstick off the mirror—for having been found out. And it was a potent one indeed!

She felt anger rising inside her, and said, 'You dare to call me insensitive, Roche Delacroix? Well, you invented the word. You bring me here—you push Solange and me together, even though it's obvious she can't stand the sight of me—and you tell me nothing— nothing!' She took an unsteady breath. 'I had to hear about Marie-Christine from a stranger—and now there's this. Your first wife nearly drowned your child —and you didn't tell me.'

'Samantha, listen to me . . .'

'No, I won't listen.' Her voice shook. 'You're the one who's cruel. You want me to be Solange's stepmother, and yet you hide all the facts that might lead to any understanding between us. I'm supposed to be your wife, but you never talk to me. In fact, you avoid me. I'm surrounded all the time by secrets that I don't understand, and when I make mistakes that could have been avoided, or jump to the wrong conclusions, I get the blame. Well, I've had enough. I can't take any more. I'm leaving Grand Cay and you can't stop me.'

Suddenly, all the misery and wretchedness of the past

days came boiling up inside her, and she lifted her hand and slapped him as hard as she could across the face. She felt his anger answer her own, as his fingers closed bruisingly round her wrist. There was retaliation in every line of his body as he jerked her towards him. With a strength she hadn't realised she possessed, she wrenched herself free and fled from him.

As if, she thought, with a sob, the devil was after her.

CHAPTER NINE

IT SEEMED an endless afternoon. Even with the shutters closed against the full blaze of the sun, Samma's room was like an oven, the heat draining her, while her mind rode an eternal weary treadmill.

She had told Roche she was leaving him, yet in practical terms how could she? He had her passport, and the amount of hard cash she possessed would buy her a ticket to nowhere.

In reality, she was no better off than she had been on Cristoforo, she thought wretchedly, but at least she'd had nothing to concern her there, except Clyde's vagaries. She had been spared the agony of heartache which was now wrenching her apart.

She was still stunned by Solange's behaviour. How could a child as young as that be capable of such duplicity? she asked herself desperately. She had not even guessed at the extent of Solange's resentment of her, and her determination to be rid of any companion foisted on her by her father.

Why hadn't she been more wary of Solange's apparent overtures? And why hadn't some instinct warned her that the child would go to any lengths necessary to force her out of Belmanoir?

Because I had this romantic notion that I would succeed where everyone else had failed, she told herself derisively. I could see us all living together, like a normal, happy family. I really thought it could happen.

But she'd underestimated all the factors against her

—Roche's passion for Elvire, Solange's malice, and above all, her own youth and inexperience.

That was all she'd ever had to offer Roche, she thought bitterly. What a fool she'd been to think it could ever be enough!

As the light began to fade from the sky, she sank into a shallow, dreamless sleep, to be awoken eventually by a touch on her shoulder. She sat up with a start to find the lamp beside the bed had been lit, and that Elvire was standing over her.

Samma sat up, pushing her hair back from her face with a gesture that was almost defiant. 'What do you want?' she asked flatly.

Elvire's brows rose slightly. 'I came to tell you that dinner is served.'

'I'm not hungry.'

Elvire studied her for a moment. 'Starving yourself, *madame,* will achieve nothing.'

'And when I want your advice I'll ask for it,' Samma returned angrily. 'Now, leave me alone, please.'

Elvire's lips tightened. 'As you wish.' She turned as if to go, then swung back again. She said with surprising energy, 'I am wrong about you, it seems, Madame Delacroix. When you came here, I thought, "That little one, she is a fighter. She will not give way." Now you talk as if you are defeated.'

Samma's lips parted in sheer astonishment as she stared up at the other girl. She said in a low voice, 'Is it really any wonder?'

Elvire sighed. 'Perhaps not. There are many obstacles in your way, of course.' She gave Samma a grave look. 'And I think perhaps that you see me as one of them.' She hesitated. 'Someone has told you, I think, of my relationship with Roche?'

Samma swallowed, wondering whether she was

dreaming. 'It wasn't really necessary,' she said awkwardly. 'I—I guessed.'

'*Vraiment?*' Elvire smiled wearily. 'We had hoped, Roche and I, that it would remain a secret. But I suppose that was too much to expect.' She shrugged. 'But I can see why you resent my presence here, although I am sorry for it. I had hoped you would be able to understand.'

Samma thought hysterically that this had to be one of the most bizarre conversations of all time.

'But you will not have to suffer me for much longer,' Elvire went on. 'I have been at Belmanoir long enough. It is time I returned to my own life.'

Samma felt as if she'd been pole-axed. She said with difficulty, 'Have you spoken to—to Roche about your plans?'

Elvire shook her head. 'Not yet. But he has always known my stay here was only temporary. He will not stand in my way.'

Samma stared at her. 'Are you quite sure of that?' She bit her lip. 'I had a different impression.'

'Ah.' Elvire's smile was tender. 'He is loyal, Roche, and very protective. When he has learned to trust again, he will be all the man any woman could want.' She sent Samma a clear-eyed look. 'And you, I think, will be able to chase the remaining shadows from his life.'

'With Solange hating me—doing anything she can to get rid of me? Like that little drama she staged earlier today?'

Elvire frowned. 'What are you saying?'

'That I was set up quite deliberately, 'Samma said stonily. 'Solange asked me to teach her to swim—almost insisted on it, then performed her panic-stricken act for her father.' She shook her head.

'Ghost messages on the mirror are one thing. This kind of malice is something else.'

Elvire's frown deepened. 'If it was true, I would agree. But a child like Solange is not capable of such conduct.'

'Oh, no?' Samma asked drily. 'And how did she put my predecessors to flight, may I ask? Conjure up *Le Diable*, or simply hit them with a hatchet?'

There was a silence, then Elvire began to laugh. 'At least you begin to sound more like yourself,' she said crisply. 'Now, come and eat, before Roxanne works herself into a frenzy.'

Samma swung herself reluctantly off the bed. She wasn't sure how it had happened, but it seemed that Elvire and she had become allies in some weird way.

'Is Solange downstairs?' she asked, as she ran a comb through her dishevelled hair.

'No. She has some sedative tablets prescribed for when the nightmares occur, so I gave her one.' Elvire paused. 'The panic was genuine, I would swear.'

'I know,' Samma said wryly. 'It just proves how far she's prepared to go to get rid of me.'

Elvire's brow was creased. 'But for someone of her age to think of such a thing . . . *Ce n'est pas possible, ça*. It makes no sense.'

Very little that's happened here does, Samma thought bitterly, as she sat in solitary splendour in the dining-room, Roxanne's splendid cooking turning to ashes in her mouth.

Not long ago, she'd been envisaging a scenario where Elvire had helped Marie-Christine to a premature death, in order to take her place. Now, suddenly, she saw the other girl as someone she might, under other circumstances, have liked—have even wanted as a friend.

Or perhaps I'm just having an identity crisis brought on by the events of the past few days, she thought, her mouth twisting.

What she could not understand was why Elvire was choosing to leave now, just when her influence over Roche had apparently never been stronger. Or had the other girl simply resigned herself to the fact that Roche would never marry her, and decided she no longer wanted a subsidiary role in his life?

And, even if she did leave, what guarantee was there that Roche would ever want Samma to take her place on any permanent basis?

Perhaps I should have been honest with her, too, Samma thought ruefully. Told her that my stay here is purely temporary as well. If I allow it to be, she amended hastily.

Perhaps Elvire was right, and she was being unnecessarily defeatist. Solange might have won the first real confrontation between them hands down, but she would never get away with that again, and Samma intended to let her know it. And as soon as possible, she decided, pushing away her coffee-cup.

There was a light burning in Solange's room. Presumably the effect of the sedative had worn off, Samma thought, as she pushed the door open and went in.

Solange, propped up by pillows, was reading a large book. She directed a sulkily suspicious glance towards her visitor. 'What do you want?'

'A few words with you,' Samma said affably, sitting down on the edge of the bed.

'I am reading.'

'So I can see. Stories about wicked stepmothers, no doubt. Well, I won't keep you from them a moment longer than necessary.' Samma paused, then said flatly, 'I just want you to know that this afternoon's performance was the final one. I was prepared to be your friend, but you've proved to me that isn't what you want.' She shrugged. '*Ça ne fait rien.* But I'm staying here, whether you want it or not, and there'll be no more phony swimming lessons, or threats from *Le Diable.*' She paused. 'Do I make myself clear?'

Solange said on a triumphant note, 'Papa was angry with you. I know he was. I heard the servants talking.'

Samma shrugged again. 'He had good reason,' she said briefly. 'After what you made him think. But there's a saying, Solange—forewarned is forearmed.'

There was uncertainty in the small face. 'What does that mean?'

'That I won't be caught again,' Samma said bluntly. 'So—forget whatever else you may be planning. Unless, of course, you want Papa to know about the tricks you have been playing.'

The book slid from Solange's hands, and she made no effort to retrieve it. She said slowly, 'You—have not told him already?'

'Of course not.' Samma stared at her. 'What do you take me for? But that little scene you played this afternoon could have had very serious consequences and . . .'

'But you did not tell him that I tricked you?' Solange persisted. 'Why not?'

'Because it's between the two of us,' Samma said crisply. 'Isn't it enough to make Papa angry with me? You don't want him cross with you as well.'

'But you want that,' Solange burst out. 'You hate me. You want me to be sent away from here—away from Papa. Do you think I am a fool—that I do not know this? You will always be jealous of me, because Papa loves me more than you, so you want to see me sent far away from Belmanoir.'

Samma felt a pang twist inside her. Roche had clearly not discussed his plans for her future schooling with his only child.

She said gently, 'Solange, I promise you that nothing could be further from the truth. Where on earth did you get the idea I wanted you sent away?'

'I have always known it. First those others—and now you. They wanted to come here—oh, you all want to come—but to be with Papa, not with me. And, now that Papa has married you, you will arrange for me to go away, so that you can have Papa all to yourself.'

Samma took the small, shaking hands in hers. She said quietly, 'Solange, who's been telling you this nonsense? Neither Papa nor I have any intention of sending you away. I came here to look after you. I've told you that.'

'Until you can persuade Papa to get rid of me.' Solange snatched her hands away.

Samma gave her an even look. 'Well, you've certainly given me sufficient cause,' she commented. 'But doesn't the fact that I haven't complained to Papa about you prove that you're wrong, and that I'm not simply looking for chances to send you away?'

The uncertainty deepened. 'I—do not know.'

'Then set that devious little mind of yours to thinking about it,' Samma advised. She got to her feet. 'And no more tricks.' She smiled briefly, and walked to the door, aware that the gaze which followed her held more bewilderment than hostility.

But this time I'm taking nothing for granted, Samma thought, as she went to her own room. Especially when I still have Roche to face.

She had no real idea what she could say to him, or

what he would even want to hear from her. After her outburst that afternoon, she'd half expected him to follow her, but she'd been left severely alone, and not long after she'd heard his car leave, presumably to take him to the casino.

And her hope that he might be home for dinner had proved a forlorn one, too.

But, if nothing else, she had to convince Roche that he couldn't send Solange away to school—show him how dependent the child was on him. And if he cynically saw her arguments as a ploy to be allowed to remain at Belmanoir herself after the agreed term, well, that was a risk she would have to take, she thought achingly.

Elvire had said she was a fighter. Well, she would battle for whatever tiny percentage of his life he was prepared to share with her.

But when dawn streaked the sky, and the room next to hers remained silent and empty, Samma realised with a sinking heart that Roche might no longer be prepared to grant her even that little. And there were tears on her face when she finally fell asleep.

Her head ached as she eventually made her way downstairs the following morning. As she reached the foot of the stairs, she heard the sound of voices coming from the dining-room.

Solange was sitting at the table, eating grapefruit, and Liliane Duvalle occupied the seat opposite, pouring coffee.

'Ah, Madame Delacroix.' She got to her feet, smiling broadly as Samma entered. 'You will forgive this informality, I know. Mademoiselle Casson gave me the impression you would not be joining us.'

Her eyes, Samma saw with distaste, were sharp with

curiosity. Clearly, it didn't take long for servants' gossip to reach Les Arbres, she thought with resignation.

She said coolly, 'I can't imagine what made her think that. *Bonjour,* Solange.'

She received in response a wary look, and a murmured greeting.

Liliane Duvalle lowered her voice confidentially. 'I came as soon as I heard of yesterday's little *contretemps.* I blame myself. I should have told you about Solange's phobia about swimming and its cause. It would have saved *la petite* a terrible ordeal.' She shook her head. 'I have been telling her that clearly you meant well, even though the outcome was unfortunate.'

'Thank you,' Samma said drily. She glanced at her stepdaughter. 'What do you say to that, Solange?'

There was a pause, then Solange said sullenly, 'It was a misunderstanding. It was not Madame's fault. She was not to blame.'

Liliane Duvalle looked frankly taken aback. 'But I understood . . .' She stopped, then shrugged briefly. 'However, one should never listen to foolish rumour. I am pleased to find you both so much in accord.'

Samma poured herself some coffee, and sat down. 'How is your research going?' she asked politely.

Liliane Duvalle threw up her hands. 'Slowly, I regret. I think my book will be a life's work—a true labour of love. Every detail I find out about *Le Diable* is so fascinating, I tend to linger over it.' She gave a musical laugh. 'A fine thing for a historian to be in love with her subject, *hein?*' She paused. 'But I forget the purpose of my visit. I wondered whether *la petite* would care to spend the day with me at Les Arbres.' She smiled at Samma. 'After all, *madame,* you are still on your honeymoon. No doubt you would welcome a chance to be relieved of your responsibilities as a stepmother, and be able to devote an entire day to your husband.'

Samma said calmly, 'It's a kind thought, Madame Duvalle, but Solange and I have plans of our own for today, haven't we, *chérie?*'

She expected to be contradicted, and was resigned to it.

There was a silence, then Solange said slowly, 'Yes, we have plans. I am—sorry, Tante Liliane.'

Liliane Duvalle shrugged, her smile undiminished. '*Ça ne fait rien.* I have been occupying myself by making some new clothes for your beautiful doll, *mon enfant.* I thought we might have had a fashion parade. But there will be other times.' She got to her feet, putting a hand lightly on Solange's hair as she passed the child's chair. 'Your new *belle-mère* takes her duties towards you very seriously, *petite.* I hope you are grateful.'

Solange muttered something ungracious and returned her attention to her grapefruit.

The dining-room door swung open to admit Elvire, carrying a large flat box tied up with ribbons.

She said, 'A messenger has just delivered this for you, *madame.*'

'For me?' Samma's brows rose. 'But I wasn't expecting anything.'

'It is a wedding present,' Solange put in. 'Open it quickly, *madame.*'

Samma complied, stripping away the ribbon ties, and lifting the lid to reveal a mass of tissue. 'What in the world . . .' She delved among the folds, and gasped. 'Oh, my goodness . . .'

It was a dress, a ripple of silk chiffon in creamy

white, its halter bodice frankly minimal, the full skirt
misted with a subtle drift of silver flowers.

Her wardrobe upstairs was full of beautiful things,
but this was different. It was flagrantly, dreamily
romantic, the shimmering slide of the material overtly
sensuous as she touched it.

'It is a bridal gown, *non?*' Solange piped, putting
out a reverent hand. 'Are you and Papa not really
married after all, *madame?*'

Samma swallowed. 'Yes,' she said quietly. 'We
are—really married, Solange.' There was a tiny
envelope in the box, and her hand shook slightly as
she reached for it, and extracted the card it contained.

It said simply, *'Forgive me—Roche.'*

'Where did it come from?' Solange asked. 'Is it a
present from Papa?'

'Yes.' Samma's mouth was dry suddenly, her heart
thudding violently.

Solange gave a rapturous sigh. 'It is so beautiful.
When will you wear it? Will it be tonight?'

Tonight. The word seemed to sing in Samma's head
with all kinds of evocative promise.

She said softly. 'Yes—oh, yes.' And thought with a
pang—If he is here to wear it for . . . As she folded the
dress back into its protective coverings, the card
slipped from her hand, and fluttered to the floor.
Samma bent to retrieve it, but Liliane Duvalle got
there first.

'Oh, la la!' She darted a smiling glance at the
message and then at Samma. 'It must have been quite
a sin to require such redemption.'

Samma felt a wave of colour sweep into her face.
She was suddenly all too aware of Elvire standing
there, a silent witness.

She said swiftly, 'Not really. A—a tiff.' She held out

her hand for the card. 'I'll take the dress upstairs.'

'Permit me, *madame*.' Elvire took the box from her, her expression impassive.

'You see, Tante Liliane,' Solange put in, 'we had our fashion parade, after all!'

'So we did, although I am afraid you will find my poor efforts bear no comparison to a *haute-couture* label.' Madame Duvalle gave Samma a knowing look. 'To be mistress of Belmanoir has many advantages, *madame*, as I am sure you are discovering.' She patted Solange's cheek. '*A bientôt, petite.*'

Solange returned, '*Au revoir,*' but it was clear her attention was still focused on the new dress. There was a slight wistfulness in her expression, which was not lost on Samma.

When they were alone, she said, 'Why don't we go and look at your clothes, Solange? And you can show me the ones you particularly like.'

Solange frowned. 'Many of them do not fit me any more,' she said.

Samma examined a fleck on her nail. 'Then perhaps we should get you some new ones,' she said. 'Where do you usually go for your things?'

'Madame Trevaux has a shop in St Laurent. Papa tells her my size, and she sends what is suitable.'

Samma digested this with an inward grimace. For a busy man, she supposed, such an arrangement might be a boon, but for a little girl . . .?

She said cheerfully, 'Well, I think it would be more fun to go into St Laurent and look round the shops for ourselves—try things on.'

Solange could not disguise the swift, excited breath she drew. 'Can we go now?'

'Why not?' Samma glanced at her watch. 'If there's a car I can drive.'

'There is,' Solange assured her. 'It is the one Elvire uses.' She gave a joyous wriggle, then sobered, sending her stepmother a speculative look. 'This is another bribe, *hein?*'

Samma met her gaze. 'No,' she said. 'No more bribes. This is just the way things are going to be from now on. You, *mademoiselle*, are stuck with me, so you may as well make the best of it.'

A curious expression crossed Solange's face, half wary, half frightened, as if something basically unwelcome had occurred to her, but before Samma could ask what was wrong she was smiling again, and the moment was lost.

The shopping trip, Samma thought cautiously, a couple of hours later, had been a modest success. When encouraged to choose for herself, Solange turned out to have an innate sense of colour, and there had been few clashes as the number of carrier bags and boxes in the car mounted. The little girl had looked wistfully at some ornately frilled dresses, but Samma and the saleswoman between them had managed to convince her that an uncluttered line was far more becoming to her.

There was relative harmony between them as they drove back to Belmanoir.

As she braked in front of the house, Samma noticed with a catch of her breath that Roche's car was parked there, too. So, he'd returned at last.

Solange flew into the house, calling to Hippolyte to come and unpack the car, and Samma followed more sedately, trying to control the sudden hammer of her pulses.

Roche emerged from the *salon*, and stood watching her. He was unsmiling, his dark gaze cool and rather questioning.

'Where have you been?'

'I was going to ask you precisely the same thing.' Her voice was faintly breathless, she realised with vexation.

He said, 'I spent the night at the casino. I needed to think.' He motioned her ahead of him into the *salon*. 'I telephoned the house an hour ago, and Elvire said you had taken Solange shopping to St Laurent.' He gave her an incredulous look. 'Is it true?'

'Quite true. I—I told them to send the bills to you. I hope that's all right.'

'Of course.' He frowned. 'But I should have made arrangements—opened an account for you to draw on.'

'There's no need. You've already been far too generous.' She sounded as stilted as a schoolgirl. She paused, taking a breath. 'The—the dress is wonderful, but there was no need . . .'

'I thought there was every need,' he said quietly. 'I have been unfair to you, *ma chère*. You made me see that, and I wished to make amends.' He paused. 'Samantha, will you have dinner with me tonight?'

She swallowed. 'Of course. Will—will you be home at the usual time?'

Roche shook his head. 'I did not mean here. There are still things I must say to you—explanations which I would prefer to make away from this house. Do you understand?' He made an impatient gesture. 'No, that is foolish. How could you?' He smiled at her gravely. 'I need to be alone with you, *mignonne*. Will you come with me?'

Swift, incredulous joy was opening inside her like a sunburst. 'If—if that's what you want,' she managed.

'It's what I want.' He walked over to her, and stood

for a moment looking down at her, at the shyness in her eyes, the betraying bloom of colour in her cheeks. He said softly, 'But not all I want, *ma belle.* From tonight there will be no more secrets—nothing to keep us apart.' He lifted a hand, and tucked a strand of hair back behind her ear. *'D'accord?'*

Samma nodded mutely, suddenly incapable of speech.

Roche bent his head and kissed her on the mouth, lightly, but with a dizzying sensuousness, his hands holding her shoulders to draw her swiftly and intimately close against him. Through the barrier of their clothes, Samma could feel the warmth of his body, the sweet yielding of her own flesh in response.

She seemed to breathe him, absorb him, wanting him as sharply and frankly as he wanted her. She knew that if he was to draw her, in that moment, down on to one of the sofas or even the floor, she would surrender to him. When he straightened, putting her away from him, her disappointment was almost painful.

He said huskily, 'Until tonight,' and left her with the echo of that promise.

CHAPTER TEN

SAMMA put the final dress on its hanger, and stood back. 'That's finished,' she said with satisfaction.

There was no reply, and she flicked a sideways glance at Solange. The child had responded with enthusiasm to Samma's initial suggestion that they should put her new things away in her room, but she'd grown more and more silent, and the familiar sulky look was now firmly in place.

Samma suppressed a sigh. 'What's the matter?' she asked directly. 'Don't you like your new clothes, after all?'

'They are beautiful,' came the grudging reply, after a pause.

'What is it, then?'

There was another silence, then Solange burst out, 'You mean to stay here at Belmanoir, don't you, *madame,* in spite of the curse?'

This time Samma sighed aloud. 'Oh, Solange, you know as well as I do that there is no curse. You invented it so you could play tricks on your companions and get rid of them.'

'A little—maybe,' Solange admitted. 'But the curse is real, and it will fall on you if you stay. It would be safer if you went now.'

In that, Samma thought wryly, she was probably quite right.

She shook her head. 'Sorry, *chérie. Le Diable* himself would have to appear and order me to walk the plank before I'd take any notice. And even then I'd probably challenge him to a duel.'

'You must not joke about such things.' Samma sudenly realised that Solange was trembling. 'You are in danger.'

'We live in a dangerous world.' Samma dropped on to her haunches beside her stepdaughter. 'Solange,' she said gently, 'you mustn't let these silly old stories get to you.'

'They are not stories,' Solange denied. 'The hating is real, and it is all around you. You must believe me.'

Samma smiled at her. 'Well, I'll believe that you believe it, and that will have to do. And now I'm going down for a swim. Care to join me by the pool?'

Solange visibly shrank, shaking her head vehemently, and Samma did not press the point. There was time, she thought. All the time in the world.

She was sorry the Delacroix curse had raised its ugly head again, she reflected as she changed in her room, but at least this time Solange had been warning her about it, instead of threatening her, which had to be a step in the right direction.

On her way downstairs, she remembered that she hadn't yet told Elvire that she and Roche would be dining out. She recalled, too, that she'd seen Elvire going towards her room in the other wing a little earlier.

She was just about to knock on the door, when she heard the unmistakable sound of deep and passionate sobbing coming from within. She stood very still for a moment, feeling slightly sick. Elvire might have declared her intention of leaving Belmanoir, but that didn't inevitably mean her love for Roche was dead.

It must hurt her, Samma decided wretchedly, to know that he's started paying attention to me. His sending me that dress must have confirmed all her worst fears. And what kind of happiness can I build with him on the foundation of someone else's misery?

She shivered. Would Elvire be always there—between them, even in absence?

One thing was certain. She couldn't disturb Elvire now that her serene mask had slipped, and she was giving way to her unhappiness and bitterness.

I'm the last person in the world she'll want to see, Samma thought, turning away. I'll speak to Roxanne instead.

But the incident cast a shadow over the afternoon, which not even swimming and sunning herself could dispel.

And, later, as she walked back to the house to begin getting ready for her dinner date with Roche, she felt that same odd conviction that someone was watching her. She halted abruptly, peering through the tall hibiscus hedges.

She said directly, 'Is someone there? Hippolyte—is that you?' But only silence answered her.

She tried to tell herself that she'd imagined it because she was on edge, but she couldn't convince herself. That awareness of prying eyes had been too strong, too definite.

As she entered the house, she could hear from the *salon* Solange's voice raised in angry, tearful protest, mingling with Roche's deeper tones, and groaned inwardly.

'What's the matter?' she asked, as she went into the room.

'You are going out tonight, and leaving me alone here. I do not wish that.' There were bright spots of colour burning in the child's cheeks.

'You grow above yourself, *mon enfant*,' Roche said

coldly. 'Understand that you do not dictate to me now or at any time.'

'But I am frightened to be alone,' Solange said, her face crumpling desolately.

'This nonsense again!' Roche raised clenched fists towards the ceiling in a gesture of total exasperation. He swung towards Samma. 'Will you please explain to this child that the possession of new clothes does not automatically grant her the right to accompany us wherever we go?'

Samma tried to pour oil on troubled waters. 'Papa and I are only having dinner together, *chérie*. Everyone in the restaurant will be grown up. You would be very bored.'

'I want to go with you,' Solange said defiantly. 'I am always being left here alone.'

Samma turned to Roche, 'Couldn't we . . .?

'No,' he said icily. 'We could not, *ma belle*. I refuse to submit to this kind of emotional blackmail from a child. Solange must learn that we need some time to ourselves, you and I.'

'But if she's frightened of being alone . . .' Samma persisted in a low voice.

Roche gestured impatiently. *'Qu'est-ce que tu as?* A houseful of servants, including Elvire, hardly implies total solitude.' He directed a minatory glance at his angry daughter. 'You are becoming spoiled, *ma petite*. I also have a claim to Samantha's time and company. She does not belong to you alone.'

'And she does not belong here, either,' Solange burst out. '*Le Diable* is going to make her sorry that she came here!' she added with a little wail, and ran out of the room.

Samma made to follow her, but Roche's hand closed on her arm.

'Leave her,' he directed curtly. 'Nothing will be gained by pandering to these tantrums of hers.'

'I suppose not.' Samma bit her lip. 'But I hate to see her so unhappy.'

Roche's lips twisted slightly. 'I see she has found the way to that soft heart of yours, *ma chère*. But you must not let her impose on you.'

Samma looked down at the floor. 'Maybe, if you gave her more of your time—behaved more warmly towards her, she wouldn't constantly seek attention like this,' she suggested in a low voice.

She expected some angry come-back but, after a pause, Roche said quietly, 'Perhaps you are right, Samantha, but it is not easy for me for all kinds of reasons. There is still so much you do not understand.'

'Then tell me,' she begged.

He lifted a hand and ran it gently down the curve of her cheek. 'Later, *mignonne*. When we are truly alone.'

And with that, she supposed, she had to be content.

Upstairs, she ran a deep, hot bath, and luxuriated in its scented water, letting the odd tensions which the day had produced drain out of her. She massaged body lotion into her glowing skin, before slipping on lacy briefs, and a matching underskirt. The design of the white dress wouldn't permit her to wear a bra.

Sitting at her dressing-table, she experimented with various ways of doing her hair, before deciding rather ruefully to allow it to swing soft and shining on her shoulders in the usual way. She took extra care with her make-up, shadowing her eyes so that they looked wide and mysterious, accentuating the warm bloom of her cheeks.

I look like a woman dressing for her lover, she

thought, and felt her entire body clench in warm, pleasurable yearning at the thought.

Barefoot, she rose, and went across to the closet to get the dress. Elvire, she thought frowningly, had not put it away with her usual care, demonstrating her emotional agitation. In fact, it was sticking out from the surrounding garments, and half off its hanger.

She thought, 'I hope it's not creased,' then stopped, a little choking cry of disbelief escaping her lips, as she saw the gaping tears and slashes all down the front which had destroyed it. The lovely filmy skirt was in rags, and the bodice had been ripped apart in total wanton devastation.

The dress fell from her shaking hands on to the carpet as nausea rose within her.

Oh, Solange—no! Please don't let it be Solange, she thought with a kind of agony.

Could this really be what the little girl's tearful, angry exit had led to? And what would Roche say when he found out?

If he found out, Samma thought, feverishly bundling the pathetic heap of fabric to the back of the wardrobe. Relations between Roche and Solange seemed strained enough. If he discovered his gift had been deliberately ruined, then his anger would be formidable, and Solange was already far too nervous and highly strung.

If that was all, Samma thought, shivering. The rips in the dress had obviously been made with a knife, or a sharp pair of scissors in a blind fury of hatred and jealousy which went beyond mere temper tantrums. Could a small girl really possess so sick and violent a mind? It didn't bear thinking about.

There was a tap on the door, and Roche said, 'Are you ready, *ma belle?*'

She clutched at the towel she was wearing draped over her bare shoulders. 'I'll be five minutes,' she called back shakily.

There was laughter in his voice, 'You are making me impatient, Samantha. Are you sure you need no assistance—with a zip, perhaps?'

'No.' She got the words out somehow. 'I can manage.'

'*Quel dommage*,' he said still laughing, and she heard his footsteps retreating.

Samma pulled out another dress at random, black, square-necked and long-sleeved. It was chic, and its stark lines added an air of fragility to her blonde looks, but it was not the dress she had dreamed all day of wearing for him, of entrancing him in so that he would forget Elvire for ever—the dress she'd imagined him removing with passionate tenderness.

When she was ready, she surveyed herself. The happy colour in her face, the light in her eyes had faded, she thought sadly. She looked strained, wary again. What was it he'd once called her? 'A little cat that has never known kindness.'

A little cat, she thought, that's been kicked too many times.

She let herself out on to the balcony and went along to Solange's room. The little girl, propped up by pillows, was reading, her face still tearstained. She glanced up with a mutinous thrust of her lower lip, as Samma walked towards her, then her face sharpened with surprise and disappointment.

'Where is your lovely dress?'

'I think you know' Samma kept her voice level. In the big bed, Solange looked so small, so fragile to have inflicted such damage.

Solange frowned. 'I do not understand.'

'Then that makes two of us.' Samma sat down wearily on the edge of the bed. She said, 'Solange, things can't go on like this. I thought we had agreed no more tricks—although what you did to my dress is worse than any trick.' She glanced round her. 'What did you use—one of the knives from the kitchen? You'd better give it back to me and . . .'

'What did I use for what?' Solange's face was small and pinched suddenly. 'The dress—something has happened to it?'

'It's cut to ribbons—totally ruined, as you very well know.' Samma swallowed. 'And this is something we can't keep between the two of us. Papa is bound to find out eventually . . .'

'You think I cut your dress? But I did not. I could not! It was so beautiful. I wanted to see you in it looking like a fairy princess. I wanted to be with you when you wore it.' The anguish in the child's voice was genuine. 'Samma, you must believe me. I would not do such a thing, even if I was angry—oh, beyond words.'

'Nevertheless, it has happened, and someone must be responsible.' Samma kept her voice level. 'Have you any idea who it could be?'

There was a perceptible hesitation, then Solange said in a half-whisper, *'Le Diable . . .'*

'Is dead,' Samma said patiently. 'My dress was damaged by someone who's very much alive.'

Solange shivered. 'But he—makes things happen, I think. I said you were in danger.'

Her gaze did not meet her stepmother's. Samma thought, She's protecting someone—she must be. Someone who established a right to her loyalty before I ever got here. But whom? Almost against her will, she remembered the sound of that desolate, bitter weeping from Elvire's room earlier. Had that lonely grief erupted into malice, and a final despairing blow against the girl who was supplanting her with Roche? It was almost as unpalatable an idea as her original fear that it might have been Solange. She got up wearily.

'We'll talk tomorrow,' she said quietly. 'Don't worry, I'll sort something out.'

Solange gave a small, reluctant nod. 'But take care,' she said in that same scared whisper.

Roche was waiting for Samma at the foot of the stairs. His brows rose in autocratic enquiry when he saw her. 'Why that dress, *ma belle*, and not the other?'

'The—the white dress needs some alteration,' Samma improvised hastily. It wasn't altogether a lie, she thought sadly.

'It does?' Roche sounded faintly surprised, then smiled reluctantly. *'Eh bien*, I am well paid for my arrogance in thinking I could gauge your size with total accuracy.' The dark eyes caressed her with disturbing warmth. 'And what does it matter? You, *mignonne*, look beautiful in anything—or nothing,' he added softly.

Swift heat invaded Samma's face, and she couldn't think of a single thing to say in reply. And the silence continued as she sat beside him in the car, as they sped towards St Laurent.

'Why so quiet?' he asked at last. 'Are you regretting your promise to dine with me?'

'Oh, no!' The denial was so immediate and vehement that she embarrassed herself.

'Then what is wrong?'

She swallowed. 'Oh—things.'

'Solange?'

Samma moved her shoulders evasively. 'Perhaps.'

He sent her a swift smile. 'I said she was not to accompany us, *ma belle*, and I meant it. I want no one in your thoughts tonight but myself.' His mouth twisted in self-deprecation. 'Desire for you makes me selfish, *chérie*.'

Her heart was beating like a drum. It was so difficult to remember she wasn't the first one he'd beguiled with that seductive tenderness in his voice. the first one to be taken to heaven or hell in his arms.

Although the hell would come later, she thought, biting her lip, when he no longer desired her.

She found a voice from somewhere. 'Where are we going?'

'To the casino. I remember you once expressed an interest in it, and I have an excellent chef there.' He shot her a glance. 'I hope you are not disappointed?'

'Not at all.' If he'd suggested a visit to the local electricity plant she would probably have been equally beguiled, she thought ruefully.

Her first sight of the casino made her gasp out loud. A great central tower, flanked by ramparts and gun emplacements, it loomed over the edge of the harbour like some predatory grey stone beast.

'What do you think?' Roche asked, as he swerved the car expertly under its gate.

'It looks more like an armed fortress than a place of entertainment,' Samma said rather dazedly, and he laughed.

'You are right, *ma belle*. It was, of course, *Le Diable's* stronghold. But these days the victims come willingly to be pirated of their loot.'

The forbidding exterior gave no clue to the luxury to be found within, Samma soon discovered. While the character of the building had been retained, no expense had been spared on the décor, and other details. It was romantically and unashamedly opulent, Samma thought, gazing upwards at crystal chandeliers, while her high heels sank into deep piled carpet.

'The gaming-rooms and the restaurant are all on the first floor,' Roche told her. 'And the administrative offices and my suite are on the next floor. We will see them later.'

There was a table awaiting them in the bar, and an attentive waiter hovering to serve drinks.

'A champagne cocktail.' Roche's smile was wicked as he handed Samma her glass. 'I thought you should know what they really taste like. Perhaps it will stop you from hurling it at me.' He ran a slow finger down the curve of her cheek. 'I am still waiting to exact my revenge for that little incident,' he murmured, and Samma's first sampling of her drink was a gulp which nearly made her choke.

When she had recovered her breath, and her equilibrium, she began to look around her, partly out of genuine curiosity, but mostly to avoid the disturbing intensity of Roche's gaze.

The restaurant lay beyond an elegantly draped archway, and Samma could see that nearly all the tables were already occupied by sleek, bejewelled women and their dinner-jacket-clad escorts. From somewhere she could hear dance music being played by a small but sophisticated combo. The whole atmosphere breathed money, and something more. There was a buzz, a genuine excitement in the air that she supposed gambling for high stakes engendered. She shrugged mentally. She herself had never been able to see the attraction, but then she'd had Clyde as an awful warning.

'What are you thinking?' Roche asked, his face quizzical.

She smiled faintly. 'Just wondering where all the rich people come from.'

'I think they flock like migrating birds from one fashionable place to another,' he said drily. 'At the moment, Grand Cay is a fashionable place.'

'And if they suddenly change their minds?'

He laughed. 'Afraid I will let you starve, *migonne?*' he mocked. 'I won't. The casino is only one of my business interests—and the least interesting. Like my black-hearted ancestor, I prefer boats.'

Samma felt a little shiver run through her. She said tautly, 'Could we leave *Le Diable* out of the conversation for once, please? I've had enough of him.'

'My own sentiments entirely. And we have other topics to discuss.' He paused. 'Samantha, do you remember my telling you early in our acquaintance that I had a mistress? It is time I explained to you exactly what I meant.'

Her mouth went dry. 'There's no need. I—I know already. You—you must know that I do.'

'What do I know?' His mouth twisted wryly. 'We are just beginning to learn about each other, *ma chère.* I did not realise you found me so transparent.'

'That's hardly the word I'd have used,' Samma said in a low voice, her gaze fixed on her barely touched drink. She took a deep breath. 'Roche—I can't—share you.'

'You will not have to,' he said softly. 'That period in my life is over. At the time it filled a need—a loneliness, or I thought it did.'

She thought, wincing, of Elvire's need, of Elvire's loneliness. Had she spoken to Roche, told him she was leaving? No more secrets, he had said, but there were still questions she dared not ask. Perhaps there always would be. Perhaps this would be the price she would pay for loving a man like Roche Delacroix.

She said huskily, 'Please can we talk about something else?'

'Later,' he said gently. 'First, we have a small matter of business to transact.' He looked past her, lifting his hand in smiling acknowledgement. As Samma glanced round, she saw Maître Giraud coming towards them.

'Madame Delacroix.' He bowed over her hand, his eyes dancing with admiration. 'You look radiant—*ravissante*. I need not ask if marriage is agreeable to you.'

Samma flushed, murmuring something in reply, while Jean-Paul turned to Roche.

'I have the papers here,' he announced, tapping the document case he was carrying. 'Have you explained your intentions to your bride?'

'Not yet.' Roche took her hand. 'I am making certain settlements on your behalf, *chérie*. It is time your finances were placed on a regular basis.'

'Is that really necessary?' she asked, unevenly.

'It is, believe me,' Jean-Paul put in. 'One must be prudent, after all, and if anything were to happen to Roche . . .'

Samma shook her head violently. 'I don't even want to think about that,' she said. 'Please—can't we leave things as they are?'

'That is impossible,' Roche told her gently. 'You are my wife, *ma belle*, and your status requires safeguards. I wish to do this for you.'

Samma looked down at the table. 'It—it wasn't in our—original agreement,' she reminded him, low-voiced.

His fingers clasped hers more strongly. 'That, I think is something we shall have to re-negotiate.'

There was a faint note of laughter in his voice. 'When the papers are signed, and we are alone.' He got to his feet. 'I suggest we waste no more time.'

Samma felt as if she was being swept away on some slow, inexorable tide.

She was trapped, she thought, between the force of her own desire, and the enigma Roche still represented. Caught, as she'd always been, between the devil and the deep sea which waited to engulf her.

I ought to run, she thought. Escape while I still have the strength—before, like Elvire, I have no pride left.

They rode up to his office suite in a streamlined lift. Roche's room was vast, dominated by a battery of television screens which provided a panoramic view of the gaming-rooms below.

'Don't you trust your staff?' Samma stared at the screens, intrigued in spite of herself at the hectic activity they displayed.

'Implicitly,' Roche returned. 'But sometimes it is possible to see trouble coming, and fend it off before it gets out of hand.' He smiled faintly. 'Hugo Baxter is only one of a breed.'

She grimaced. 'I suppose so.'

Maître Giraud was spreading papers across the big desk. Obediently she signed where she was told, a little alarmed by the sums of money she saw mentioned. Roche added his own signature almost negligently, then opened the bottle of champagne which had been waiting in its cooler.

'To marriage,' he said lifting his glass.

Jean-Paul laughed. 'That is one toast I never expected to hear you make, *mon vieux*.'

A buzzer sounded, and Roche walked round his desk to flick an intercom switch.

He said brusquely, 'I thought I had made it clear I did not wish to be disturbed . . .' He listened frowningly, then sighed. 'Very well, I will come down.'

'Problems?' Jean-Paul asked.

'A request for credit which my house manager does not feel equal to refusing,' Roche said, with a touch of grimness. 'Entertain Samantha until I return, *mon ami.*'

'With the utmost pleasure,' Jean-Paul said promptly, refilling Samma's glass with champagne.

She sipped slowly, assimilating more of her surroundings. Long windows had been opened to the warm night, and a table set with snowy linen and silver cutlery had been placed in front of them. Roche intended them to dine up here, it seemed. And on the other side of the room was a door, half-opened, and affording an unmistakable glimpse of a bed, with its covers invitingly turned down.

'A true home from home,' Jean-Paul commented laconically, following the direction of her gaze.

She swallowed some more wine. 'I—suppose so. And Roche did live here, didn't he?'

'At one time,' Jean-Paul agreed. 'In the bad days which are now, I hope, gone forever.' He paused. 'I will be frank. I was—alarmed by this hasty marriage of yours. Roche and I have been friends for years, and I could not bear it if he made another mistake, but seeing you together has allayed my fears completely.' He sighed slightly. 'In fact, I am almost tempted to try my own luck again.'

'You're not married?' Samma was frankly surprised. Jean-Paul was clearly affluent, ambitious and with more than his fair share of attraction.

There was a silence, then he said slowly, 'At one time I hoped to be, but the woman I loved would not have me. There was, she considered, an impediment which her pride would not allow her to ignore. I was young and intolerant, and we—parted.'

'I'm sorry,' Samma said with sincerity.

'I was a fool,' he said, with a shrug. 'I should have overruled her, swept her off her feet. I see her now from time to time, and I know that for me it is still the same, but for her—who can say?'

He smiled at Samma. 'Perhaps I should engage you, Madame Delacroix, to plead my cause—to convince her that love is real, and marriage can still bring joy.'

She flushed. 'I think I should have to be married for much longer to sound really convincing.' Wanting to change the subject, she went on, 'Those awful people—the Augustins—did they leave?'

'*Mais oui,* and if God is good they will never return,' Jean-Paul said with a sigh. 'All you have to do, *madame,* is stay married to Roche. If you decided to leave him, it might be a different story.'

Samma set her glass down slowly on the desk, aware of an odd sinking sensation deep inside her. 'You mean—if Roche and I separated, they would try again for custody of Solange?'

'*Certainement.*' He smiled at her. 'But I have it on the best authority that your husband has not the slightest intention of letting you go, so be warned.'

'He told you so?' Her heart was thudding unsteadily, and the palms of her hands felt damp.

'Only yesterday,' he said casually. 'He admitted to me, as a friend, you understand, that he would do anything to keep you at his side.' He sighed again. 'That is love, *n'est-ce pas?*' He paused. 'Some more champagne?'

'No—thank you,' Samma managed. She felt sick suddenly—sick and bitterly humiliated. Everything Roche had said, everything he'd done, was revealed in a new and shaming light.

And she'd fallen for it, she thought despairingly. She'd allowed herself to believe that he was beginning to care for her—let herself be seduced with the promise of love—without seeing the harshly cynical motivation which had prompted his advances to her.

I saw only what I wanted to see, she thought, as pain lashed at her.

Jean-Paul was staring at her. 'Are you well, *madame?* You are very pale.'

Out of a constricted throat, she managed, 'It's a little warm in here, and I'm not used to champagne.'

Jean-Paul moved purposefully towards the intercom. 'I will call Roche.'

'No—please. I—I don't want to worry him. I think I'd better go back—to Belmanoir.' She moistened dry lips with the tip of her tongue. She started for the door, then stopped as it opened, and Roche came in.

'*Mon Dieu,* what a scene!' he said ruefully. '*Mignonne,* I'm sorry. I have been neglecting you again, in spite of my guarantee earlier.' He gave her a close look. 'Is something wrong?'

'She seems to be a little faint,' Jean-Paul said concernedly. 'Shall I fetch someone?'

Roche shook his head. 'I will look after her.' He turned to Samma. 'You are probably just hungry, *ma belle.* I will tell them to serve dinner at once.'

It would be so easy to tell herself that the gentleness in his voice was genuine—so easy, and so totally, fatally stupid. She'd been on the verge of making a complete and pathetic fool of herself, yet again. She should be thankful she'd been spared that humiliation at least.

She heard Jean-Paul say something tactful about leaving them together, and then, at long last and all too late, they were alone.

CHAPTER ELEVEN

'WHAT is it, *ma belle?*' His voice and face tender, Roche drew Samma into his arms, tensing when he felt her instinctive recoil. '*Mon Dieu,* you cannot be frightened of me! There is no need, I swear. I will be gentle . . .'

'No,' Samma said hoarsely. 'You're not going to touch me. You're not going to come near me.'

'*Chérie,* what is this? *Qu'est-ce que tu as?*' He stared at her. 'Are you really ill? Shall I send for a doctor?'

She said, 'I'm not ill. I may have been blind for a time, but that's over now.'

Roche flung his head back. 'And what does that mean?' he asked evenly.

She walked over to the desk, where the settlement papers were still lying, as she said, 'You've been very generous today, Roche, but there was no need.' She picked up the papers and tore them across, again and again. She went on, 'I've no doubt you'd have been equally generous in bed. That was the new deal, I take it—the re-negotiation you mentioned. Cash, and——' her voice faltered slightly '—and sex to keep me sweet —to keep me on Grand Cay—because if I left you, the Augustins would make another claim for Solange—and with two failed marriages behind you, Judge Lefèvre might take a different view next time.' She took a deep breath. 'Isn't that how it was?'

He said harshly, 'You seem to have it all worked out, *ma belle.* You tell me.'

It was an effort to meet the blaze of anger in his face

without quailing, but Samma bravely continued, 'But you had no need to go to those lengths. As I told you on *Allegra,* I'm here because I feel so sorry for your little girl. Your—money—a relationship—they never mattered. I never wanted either.' The words were like knives, twisting in her. 'I—I know I threatened to leave, but that was in the heat of the moment. I would have changed my mind—for Solange's sake. There was no necessity for a full-scale seduction, with financial inducements. I'll stay anyway—but without the money.' In spite of herself, her voice shook. 'And without you.'

The anger in him was almost tangible. He said too quietly, 'You are so sure the choice is yours to make?'

His hands reached for her, took her before she could back away. Her protesting cry was smothered by the heated violence of his mouth. Her hands rained blows on his chest, until he dragged her so close that her clenched fists were trapped against the hardness of his body, making further resistance an impossibility.

A lifetime ago, he'd teased her—excited her with the possibility of exacting some sensual vengeance from her. Now this had become an angry, terrifying reality. There was no more laughter, no more tenderness —just a stark and ruthless passion intent on enforcing submission, however reluctant.

When at last he lifted his head, she was weak and trembling in his arms, panic turning her limbs to water.

He said with dangerous softness, 'I brought you here to make love to you, my lovely wife, and I shall do so, with or without your permission. You will understand, I am sure, that I cannot promise under the circumstances to show you the understanding and forbearance that I once intended.' He shrugged. 'But as you do not want me anyway, what difference can it make?'

He swung her up into his arms, and carried her into the other room, tossing her contemptuously across the bed. He shrugged off his jacket, dropping it to the floor, and tugged at his black tie.

He said icily, 'If you wish to have a dress fit to go home in, *madame*, I suggest you remove it now.'

Her voice was shaking uncontrollably now, as she saw the abyss which had opened in front of her. 'Roche—please. You don't really want me—you know that . . .'

'How can I know?' His lip curled as he unbuttoned his shirt and stripped it off. 'You have been so sparing with your favours, *mignonne*. You have made me—curious, if nothing else. Now strip, before I do it for you.'

He meant it. She could see it in the smouldering light in his eyes, the harsh set of his jaw.

She gave a little sob, and fumbled for her zip.

In the other room, a telephone began to ring suddenly with loud, jarring insistence. Roche paused in his undressing, and a small, silent sigh of relief rose within her, but after a brief, furious glance in the direction of the desk, he evidently decided to ignore the interruption.

He said coldly, 'You are keeping me waiting.'

She said, 'The phone . . .'

'Can go to hell.' He smiled at her without amusement. 'I gave orders for my—night of love—to be without interruption.'

'But it could be important . . .' The pleading in her voice was unmistakable.

'Nothing, *ma belle*, could match the importance of having you—at last.' His tone jeered at her, made light of the sacrifice of her innocence.

He sat down on the bed beside her, his fingers wrenching at her zip. The dress fell away, and she felt his mouth caressing the nape of her neck, his fingers tracing the long, naked length of her back. Felt the unbidden quickening of her own flesh in response to his touch. Felt all the agony of a need she could not deny.

Very slowly, she turned to him, aware of the flame of his eyes touching her bare breasts. His hands took her shoulders, pushing her back against the pillow, and she made no resistance, her lips parting achingly as he bent over her. She knew the warmth of his breath on her face, the brush of his naked flesh against her own as he came down to her, and a little sigh, half yearning, half capitulation escaped her.

For a long moment, he looked into her widening eyes, then he said with cold mockery, 'And yet you tell me you don't want me.'

He lifted himself away from her, and walked into the other room to the desk, and the clamouring telephone. As if from a great distance, Samma watched him lift the receiver, heard him say curtly, '*Oui?*'

She saw the fierceness fade from his face, to be replaced with concern, as he said swiftly, 'Elvire—*c'est toi?* At this hour? What is wrong?'

But of course, thought Samma, who else could it possibly be? I suppose I should be—grateful . . .

She pulled her dress back into place, fastened it, found her shoes, and was past him and at the door of the office almost before he seemed aware of her presence.

She heard him say her name sharply, but she didn't even pause, running down the corridor towards the lift.

She had a breathing space. Apart from his conversation with his mistress, Roche would hardly be likely to pursue her through the casino next door to naked.

As the lift reached the ground floor, she forced herself to walk without hurrying to the main entrance.

The uniformed commissionaire touched his cap respectfully.

'*Bonsoir, m'dame.* Can I help you?'

'I would like a cab,' she said. 'Is that possible?'

'But of course.' He put his fingers to his lips and whistled, and one of the local taxis appeared as if from nowhere.

'On Mist' Roche's account, boy,' the commissionaire instructed as he opened the door and helped Samma into the car. He paused. 'Where are you going, *m'dame?*'

There was nowhere. No sanctuary—no safe refuge. No escape.

She said wearily, 'Take me to Belmanoir.'

All the lights seemed to be pouring out of the house as the cab drew up outside.

Samma hurried up the steps. She'd hoped to make her return under the cover and privacy of darkness, but even that was being denied her, she thought bitterly.

As she walked in through the door, Elvire came to meet her, her face strained.

'So you have come—thank God!' She stared past Samma. 'But where is Roche?'

Samma shrugged. 'At the casino, I suppose. You spoke to him last.'

'You mean, he has not come with you to search?' Elvire looked shaken—almost appalled.

'Search for what?'

'He did not tell you? *Mon Dieu,* it is beyond belief.' Elvire ran distracted fingers through her hair. 'Solange is not in her room. She has vanished—God alone knows where.'

'Vanished?' Samma echoed dazedly. 'But that's impossible. She's playing one of her tricks—hiding somewhere to wind us all up.'

'We have searched the house, all of us, and Hippolyte has been through the grounds three times.'

Samma felt sick suddenly. 'The pool?'

Elvire put a hand on her arm. 'He looked there first.'

'Could she have gone to Les Arbres to see Madame Duvalle?'

'I have been telephoning the house, but there is no answer.' There was a silence, then Elvire said with a little wail, 'Oh, why should she do such a thing?'

Samma felt heat burn into her face. 'She may be feeling guilty. My new dress was cut to pieces earlier, and I let her know I thought she was to blame. She swore she wasn't responsible, but perhaps . . .'

Elvire gave her an astonished look. 'Your dress? But that is impossible! She has no reason . . .'

'Except that she hates me—that she wants me gone from here.'

'Are you so sure? I had thought things were better between you.' Elvire paused. 'Show me this dress.'

In Samma's room, she stood staring at the deep slashes which mutilated the fabric from neckline to hem. At last, she said positively, 'Solange did not do that. Physically, it is not possible. The rail is high, and she could not have reached to make cuts as long as these.'

'Yet someone did.' Samma's voice shook. 'Someone

else who hates me. Was it you, Elvire?' She saw a look
of blank amazement enter the other girl's eyes, and
hurried on, 'I wouldn't blame you, if it was. You
think I'm a rival, don't you? But I'm not. Roche
doesn't really want me. I threatened to leave him, you
see, and he thought if he was—nice to me, I could be
persuaded to stay.' She bit her lip. 'But that's
all—sorted now. So there's no reason for you to leave.
I'm just staying here to—look after Solange. Roche
and I—there's nothing,' she added on a pitiful little
rush of words.

There was a long, tense silence. Elvire stood,
staring at Samma, as taut as a bowstring, a small
muscle moving in her throat.

Finally, she said, her voice breaking, 'Ah,
Dieu—you little fool! You think then that Roche and
I . . .?' She groaned. 'But it is impossible. You said
you knew—that you understood. I thought that when
Solange spoke about the portraits of the Delacroix
women you must have guessed—seen the resemblance, somehow. I told Roche that you knew the
truth—and all the time you thought that we . . .' She
gave a strained laugh. 'Blame my pride, Samantha.
The devilish Delacroix pride. I sometimes think that
is the real curse *Le Diable* bestowed on our family.'

Samma said shakily, 'Delacroix—you're a
Delacroix?'

Elvire nodded. 'Roche's—half-sister. His father was
mine, too—something I have always hated—resented.
Something I have always tried to conceal.'

'But why?' Samma's head was reeling. 'There's no
real stigma these days . . .'

'You think not? Well, *peut-être* in a more open
society—but this is a small island. My mother came to
Belmanoir as a nurse to care for Madame Delacroix

after her accident. Antoine Delacroix was lonely—desperate. He loved his wife, and had been warned that because of her injuries they might never again enjoy a normal relationship. My mother was beautiful, and they were much in each other's company. It was inevitable, I suppose, that they should become lovers. At the very time my mother became pregnant, Mathilde Delacroix began to recover, and Maman was sent away. Antoine provided money, of course, but he never saw Maman again. He never acknowledged me, although before he died he told Roche of my existence. Roche sought me out, and befriended me. He wanted to claim me openly as his sister, but I would not allow it. I told him I wanted no part of the Delacroix name—that no one must ever know, unless I gave permission.' She gave Samma a rueful look. 'Not even you, *madame, ma belle-soeur.*'

'Did you never tell anyone?' Samma shook her head in disbelief.

'Only one—the man who wished to marry me. He comes from an old and distinguished family—and had an important career in front of him. He needed a wife with advantages, not from a background as questionable as mine, so I refused him, and left Grand Cay. I threw myself into my own work—did too much, and suffered a mental crisis. Roche brought me back here to recuperate and rest. As I recovered, Marie-Christine arrived, and I agreed to stay and nurse her back to some kind of sanity and sobriety.' She paused, with a sigh. 'As you know, I failed.'

Samma stared at her. 'It was Jean-Paul Giraud, wasn't it—the man you loved?'

Elvire gave a constricted smile. 'This time you have guessed correctly. Bravo.'

'It was no guess. It was something he said himself.'

Samma swallowed. 'He—he's still in love with you. Do you know that?'

Elvire was very still for a moment. Then she said, very quietly, 'But nothing has changed. I am still Antoine Delacroix's bastard daughter—and of mixed race, besides. He would be mad to take me. I would be cruel to allow it.'

Samma said with a catch in her voice, 'That's something open to debate, I suspect. But what we have to do now is find Solange.' She looked at the slashes in the dress, and dropped the garment to the floor with an open shudder. 'And quickly.'

They searched the house again, calling the child's name, coaxing and cajoling her to come out of hiding, but there was no reply. Then they went out into the gardens with torches, and hunted again.

'Where's Mist' Roche?' Hippolyte asked Samma, as they made yet another fruitless circuit of the pool. 'Why's he not here, *m'dame?*'

Samma stifled a sigh. 'I wish I knew, Hippolyte.' She had rarely felt so frightened and so helpless. Solange seemed to have vanished into thin air, and she didn't know where to look next. Could Solange have set off on foot for St Laurent to find them, in defiance of her father's ban?

Surely not, Samma thought. Yet—she was frightened. She said she didn't want to be left here.

She stood staring into the darkness, realising with a start just what had attracted her attention.

'Hippolyte—I can see lights in the distance. What are they?'

'Oh, that's Les Arbres, *m'dame.*'

Samma said slowly, 'Is it so close? I didn't realise.' But if there were lights at Les Arbres it meant that Liliane Duvalle had returned. She and Solange were close. Maybe she would have some idea what had happened to the child . . . She stopped suddenly as a thought, totally unwelcome in its novelty, occurred to her.

She said, 'How do I get to Les Arbres, Hippolyte? Isn't there a short-cut through the gardens?'

'*Oui, m'dame.*' He pointed. 'Along the edge of the old plantation, where the slave cabins used to be.' He gave her a doubtful glance. 'Shall I come too?'

'No,' she said steadily. 'I'll find it. You concentrate on looking closer to home, Hippolyte. This is a long shot.'

Her torch was powerful, and lit the way well enough. Samma ran at a steady jog-trot, her brain teeming as it examined a new and frightening possibility.

Liliane Duvalle, she thought, the close neighbour, and family friend, whose obsession with *Le Diable* equalled Solange's. Who came and went at Belmanoir pretty much as she pleased. Whose presence would probably not even be remarked upon, if noticed. Who had been, on her own admission, a constant visitor to Marie-Christine, and knew of her predilection for vodka.

Oh God, she thought. Tell me I'm wrong. I *must* be wrong!

But, the more she thought about it, the more hideously possible it seemed. She had allowed herself to become so obsessed with Elvire that it had not occurred to her there was another young, attractive woman nearby with whom Roche might have been involved. A woman who might feel injured when supplanted by a younger rival.

She was breathless by the time she reached the house. The light she'd noticed was coming from one of the ground-floor rooms. She made herself slow down, and move quietly.

There was no point, after all, in barging in, making wild accusations which she could not substantiate.

Hearing the murmur of voices, Samma flattened herself against the wall before allowing herself a cautious peep through the open window.

The first person she saw was Solange, crouching, in a big chair. Her eyes were like saucers, her small face pinched and sallow.

She could not see Liliane Duvalle, but she could hear her voice, soft and terrifyingly normal. 'But we are friends, *mon enfant*. That girl is not your friend. She is your enemy.'

Solange swallowed. 'She talks like my friend. She is kind to me. She says she will not send me away.'

'That is what she tells you now, but I know. Tante Liliane has always been right about the women your papa has brought to Belmanoir. They want him—they want his money, but they do not want you, *petite* Solange. Trust me, *chérie*. We will get rid of this woman, as we have the others. She has been clever. She has defied us, but we will win in the end.'

Solange shook her head. 'I do not want to win,' she said defiantly. 'I do not want Samma to go. I like her.'

Liliane Duvalle chuckled quietly. 'So much the worse for both of you,' she said. 'If she stays, she will be sorry. Her dress is only the beginning.'

As Madame Duvalle moved into sight, Samma bit back a cry. The older woman was holding Solange's doll in one hand, and a pair of sharp, long-bladed scissors in the other.

As Samma watched in horror, the scissors slashed at the doll until the long blonde hair fell to the floor in ragged chunks.

'How beautiful will you be then, Madame Delacroix?' Liliane Duvalle said, and laughed.

From somewhere, Samma found the energy to move. She was through the half-open front door, and into the room before she'd even had a chance to consider what strategy she could employ. All she could think of was Solange's safety.

Solange screamed her name, and Liliane Duvalle swung round, her murderous scissors poised above the doll's face.

She smiled gaily. 'All the better,' she said. 'The pretty doll in reality.' And came towards Samma, the blades upraised.

Samma felt frozen. She put out her hands to block the other woman's advance. My face, she thought, I must protect my face! And she was aware, as if in a dream, of hands gripping her waist, lifting her out of harm's way.

Roche said grimly. 'Put the scissors down, Liliane.'

She stopped, staring at him, her face relaxing into warmth and charm.

She said with a little sigh, 'Roche—*mon amour*. You have come to me at last, as I knew you would. I've wanted you for so long—offered myself so many times.' Her voice dropped confidentially. 'But I always knew that one day you would realise that we were meant for each other—why I could not allow any other woman to have you.'

She laughed suddenly, stridently. 'That drunken fool who called herself your wife was easy. I used to visit her—bring her little gifts—in bottles—tell her stories about the past. How alarmed she used to get—and the more disturbed she was, the more she drank.' She tutted. *'Quel dommage!'*

Roche said quietly, 'And the day she died——'

'I had visited her—talked with her.' She giggled. '*Pauvre* Marie-Christine—she really believed the curse was about to fall on her. I made sure she had the car keys, then later I came back. I even drove with her for part of the way, until we reached a suitable place, then I let her take the wheel, and I—watched.'

She looked past him to Samma. 'And this child you have brought to Belmanoir.' She touched the mutilated doll with her foot. 'Will you want her, I wonder, when I have finished with her?'

He said steadily. 'I want her, and I want my daughter, Liliane. I will not allow you to hurt either of them.'

Her smile vanished. Her voice high-pitched, she said, 'Daughter? You have no daughter. Marie-Christine told me so—told me all kinds of things. How she'd made a fool of you—made you think you were marrying an innocent virgin, when all the time she was carrying another man's child.' She sent Solange a venomous look. 'Why do you keep her with you? You know you don't love her—that you can hardly bear to look at her.'

Roche said quietly, 'Marie-Christine lied to you, Liliane. She was my wife, and Solange is my child.' He put out his hand. 'Come to me, *petite.*'

'No—send her away. There can only be the two of us.' Madame Duvalle's scissors fell from her hand, as she dropped to her knees in front of him. She flung her arms round his legs, burying her face against his thighs. 'Send them all away. Love me—only me!'

The harsh, grating sound of her sobbing filled the room. In a way, it was worse than any of the threats and revelations which had gone before, Samma thought, nausea rising in her throat. As Solange ran to her, she seized the child and held her tight, aware that

Elvire and Hippolyte were in the doorway.

She whispered, 'Get a doctor,' and saw Hippolyte fade away.

Elvire walked forwards and picked up the scissors, sliding them into her pocket. She said gently and calmly, 'Get up, *madame*. You need to rest.'

Liliane Duvalle looked up at her, her face blotched with weeping. 'But I have a rendezvous,' she said with total reason. 'A rendezvous with *Le Diable*. I have been waiting for him all my life, and now he is here with me.'

'He is waiting in your room,' Elvire said. 'Come with me now, and you will find him.'

Slowly, Liliane Duvalle got to her feet, and Elvire led her away.

Roche's face was grey as he watched them go. '*Dieu!*' he said unsteadily. 'When I think what could have happened . . .' He turned on Samma. 'I searched the casino for you, *madame*,' he told her grimly. 'It was fortunate I was able to reach you in time to save you from the consequences of your own folly, once I discovered where you had gone.'

'Tante Liliane came into my room, Papa,' Solange said in a small voice. 'She made me go with her. I did not want to, but she told me *Le Diable* would take me away if I stayed.'

'*Le Diable* is a story, *petite*,' Roche said gently. 'And stories cannot hurt you any more.'

'But he seemed real,' Solange said. 'He wanted me to do things to send Samma away—like pretending to drown so that you would be angry, and blame Samma. But I did not spoil the dress.'

Roche's brows snapped together. 'What is this?'

Samma bit her lip. 'The white dress you gave me. I found it cut to pieces in my room.'

Roche drew a deep breath. 'And did not tell me?'

'Samma thought I had done it, Papa. She did not want you to be cross with me. She did not tell you about the other things, either.' Solange's face was piteous suddenly. 'Papa, why did Tante Liliane say I was not your daughter?'

Roche's face softened. 'She made a mistake, *chérie*. You are my own, all my own.' He held out his arms, and she ran to him, her face transfigured as he swung her up, cradling her against his chest. Samma felt swift tears prick at her eyes. 'Now you must go home to bed.'

'I will go with Samma,' Solange said graciously. 'Will you come too, Papa?'

He shook his head, as he set the child on her feet. 'I must wait here for the doctor.'

'Is Tante Liliane sick?' Solange asked doubtfully.

Roche touched her cheek. 'Yes, *chérie*. More sick than any of us realised, but she will be better soon. Go now.'

Solange trotted obediently out of the room, but Samma lingered, her eyes searching her husband's averted face.

She said unhappily, 'Roche—I owe you an apology. I've jumped to many conclusions—made so many mistakes . . .'

'So I learn from Elvire.' His voice was a stranger's. 'I too am sorry, *madame*, for the grave mistake I made in bringing you here.' He shrugged. 'But fortunately, it can be corrected.'

She stared at him. 'I don't understand. I'm trying to put things right between us . . .'

His eyes swept over her in icy appraisal. 'And I am telling you, *madame*, that you are free to go—to leave Grand Cay. And the sooner the better,' he added, and walked out of the room.

CHAPTER TWELVE

SAMMA lay on the pool lounger, gazing sightlessly at the endless blue of the sky. She felt half-dead, but was it any wonder? she thought restlessly. Few of them had got much sleep the previous night.

There had been a hasty conference in the *salon* at Belmanoir, attended by the doctor, a startled Jean-Paul Giraud, and a quietly spoken, middle-aged man, who turned out to be Grand Cay's top policeman.

Liliane Duvalle had been removed by ambulance to a clinic in St Laurent, and placed under sedation. Efforts would be made to find her remaining relatives in France, and arrange repatriation as soon as she was well enough to travel. No charges of any kind would be preferred against her.

'At the moment she is inhabiting a fantasy world,' Dr Barras told them gravely. 'Her admission of involvement in the death of the late Marie-Christine Delacroix may be true, or simply part of that fantasy. At the moment, it is impossible to say.' He hesitated. 'And to supply an alcoholic woman with vodka is only a moral crime.'

'I blame myself,' Roche declared bitterly, dull colour staining his face. 'I should have realised that she was becoming obsessed with *Le Diable*—with me —and taken some avoiding action. But to me, she was nothing more than a neighbour who was sometimes a nuisance.' His flush deepened. 'Whose—attentions could sometimes be embarrassing.'

'*Mon pauvre.*' Elvire patted him on the shoulder.

'She did throw herself at you, then?'

His mouth tightened. 'Yes, even before Marie-Christine's return.'

Samma found her voice. 'How did she get into the house, and into my room in particular, without being seen?'

Roche did not answer or even look at her, and it was left to Elvire to explain, 'There is an old fire escape at the corner of the balcony. It is half hidden by the vine, and one tends to forget it is there. It seems she used that, especially when she used to visit Solange at night to give her *Le Diable's* latest instructions.'

Samma shuddered. 'That would explain the nightmares. And the fact that sometimes I felt I was being watched.'

The quiet man said, 'You are fortunate, Madame Delacroix, that she did nothing but look until this evening, and that your husband arrived in time to protect you.'

I almost wish he hadn't, Samma thought. If Liliane had plunged those scissors into me, I couldn't hurt more than I do now.

Elvire got to her feet. 'Poor creature,' she said soberly. 'In spite of what she has done, I pity her.' She paused. 'Now, shall we all have some coffee?'

As she'd left the room to fetch it, Samma saw Jean-Paul slip out after her. Perhaps some good will come out of all this after all, she thought.

She had gone to her room shortly afterwards, and lain awake, straining her ears for any sound of Roche coming to bed. But yet again, the adjoining room had not been used.

Samma sighed. Well, at least she knew that the nights when he'd been absent had not been spent with Elvire, she thought, her mouth twisting. But she was no wiser about where he'd actually been, and perhaps she never would be.

She bit her lip. She felt like someone under sentence of death, with no idea when the axe might fall. Roche had already left for the day when she'd arrived downstairs.

But, on the positive side, Solange seemed to have had no trouble in recovering her spirits this morning, and was inclined to make a heroine of herself—a leaning which Samma and Elvire, in concert, had dealt with firmly and succinctly. Hippolyte had then driven her to St Laurent to spend the day with a friend.

'Will you mind being alone?' Solange had asked Samma almost anxiously before she left. 'I will come back this afternoon.' There was a long pause. 'Perhaps, this time, I may learn to swim.'

Samma smiled, smoothing the child's hair back from her face. 'There's no rush,' she said gently.

How could there be, she thought bitterly, when she might not even be there when Solange got back?

She heard a footfall on the path, and sat up hastily, hoping against hope . . . Instead, she saw Jean-Paul Giraud walking towards her, his usual smile markedly absent.

Her heart sank. 'Good—good afternoon,' she managed.

'*Bonjour, madame.* I hope you have recovered from your ordeal.' His tone was as formal as his face.

'I—I think so.'

'Excellent,' he said too heartily, and there was a silence. Eventually he said awkwardly, 'Madame Delacroix—Samantha—you must know why I am here. Roche has instructed me to arrange your departure from Grand Cay. I have been able to obtain you a

flight to the United Kingdom tomorrow.' He delved
in his briefcase, and brought out a bulging envelope.
'I have your ticket here, also your passport, and some
money in cash to deal with—immediate needs,
although Roche has asked me to assure you that your
original agreement with him still stands.' He paused.
'He told me you would understand what he meant.'

'Yes,' she said, dry-mouthed. 'Couldn't he have
given me these things himself?'

Jean-Paul's awkwardness increased. 'He—he feels it
is better if you do not meet again. He intends to
occupy his suite at the casino in the meantime.' There
was another silence, then he burst out, '*Madame*—
Samantha—none of this makes any sense. Last night
you were two people passionately in love. Today—it is
over.'

Samma bent her head. She said quietly, 'Roche
thought he was buying me, but I wasn't for sale.
There was—no love in it. Roche has always been
involved with someone else.'

'Roche has?' Jean Paul stared at her, open-mouthed.
'But that is impossible.' He gave a very Gallic shrug.
'Oh—there have been—encounters over the years. He
is a man, after all—but an *affaire* of the kind you
mention—by no means.'

Samma bit her lip. 'He told me himself he had a
mistress.'

Jean-Paul began to laugh. 'He said that—*oh, la la!* It
is a joke of ours—about the casino and his other
businesses. I reproached him once years ago because
there was no woman in his life, and he said, "My
work is my mistress, *mon vieux,* and a jealous one. I
have no time for any other." ' He stared at her. 'And it
is for this you have quarrelled?'

'No.' Samma shook her head wearily. 'That's the

least of it.'

'Ah,' he said. 'Then I am truly sorry.' He glanced around casually. 'Is Elvire in the house?'

'Almost certainly.' She forced a smile. 'Why don't you go and find her?'

When she was alone, she sat staring at the envelope, fighting back her tears. So that was it. She was being flung out of his life as suddenly as she'd been dragged into it. And with no chance of a reprieve.

She threw her head back defiantly. Well, she was damned if she'd be—dismissed like this! There were still too many things left unsaid between them, and Roche clearly intended they should stay that way.

But maybe this time it was *his* turn not to have a choice.

She picked up the envelope, and went up to the house. Jean-Paul's car was standing in the drive, the keys in the ignition. She glanced down at herself. Her pale lemon sundress was respectable enough for a trip to St Laurent, and Jean-Paul would hopefully be too occupied with Elvire to notice his car was missing for quite some time. Therefore . . .

She opened the driver's door and slid behind the wheel. The car started at the first attempt, and she set off down the drive.

The casino was once again a hive of activity when she arrived, but this time only the cleaners and staff were involved. She received a few curious glances, but it was clear she was recognised because no one challenged her as she walked to the lift, and rode up to the administrative floor.

She went straight to Roche's office, and walked in without knocking. He was sitting behind that massive desk, staring down at some papers, an open whisky bottle and a half-filled glass in front of him.

Without looking up, he said harshly, 'Hélène, I told you I would buzz if I needed you. Now leave me alone.'

She said, 'But I'm not Hélène.'

His head lifted sharply, and his expression hardened, but not before she'd glimpsed the bleakness, the vulnerability in his face.

He said glacially, 'What are you doing here? Did you not get my message?'

'Every detail of it.' She put the envelope down on the desk. 'And your little package deal. But aren't you forgetting something?'

'I don't think so. But no doubt you are going to tell me.'

'The reason I came here,' she said brightly. 'Solange, even though she isn't really your daughter at all, is she?'

'No.' His voice was stark. 'Liliane's story was true in every respect. Marie-Christine was a whore who needed a husband. She had a beautiful face and a good body, which I was not permitted to enjoy until after our wedding. That night, having had too much to drink, she gigglingly confided to me that she had already had a lover who was married, and was three months pregnant by him. She seemed to think I was so consumed by passion for her that I would overlook so small a detail. She soon discovered her mistake.'

'And the Augustins didn't know?'

'It seems not, or they would have used the information.' He gave her a long look. 'But make no mistake, Samantha. The lack of a blood tie makes no difference. Solange needs me, and I have given her my name.'

'Then having gone to all this trouble to stake your claim, I'm surprised you want to jeopardise everything now by sending me away. If the Augustins try again, you could lose her.'

'Then that is a risk I will take.' He paused. 'It does not weigh on me as heavily as the knowledge that if you remain on Grand Cay, I shall almost certainly rape you, and end up loathing myself for ever.' He gave her a blazing look. 'There, you have heard me admit it.' He pointed. 'The door is behind you. Use it.'

Her heart had begun to beat slowly and loudly. She said, 'I'll leave when I'm ready. You made me come here—deceived me in all kinds of ways—disrupted my life. I think I'm entitled to some compensation.'

'There is cash enclosed with your ticket.'

'But hardly enough to make up for some of the things I've been made to suffer since I came here.'

His mouth curled. 'Last night, *madame,* you threw my money in my face, with the accusation that I was buying you in some way. Naturally, I hesitated to insult you again.'

'I wouldn't be insulted—as I'm leaving, anyway.'

'Very well,' Roche said after a pause. He pushed back his chair, and walked to the wall behind his desk, touching a concealed switch. A section of panelling slid back to reveal a wall safe. 'How much do you want from me?'

She said huskily, 'A very great deal—but I think I'd prefer to be paid in kind, rather than cash.' She turned and walked across the room to his bedroom. 'You may leave your clothes on that chair,' she added over her shoulder.

She stood, her back turned, staring down at the bed, her stomach churning in mingled excitement and trepidation. She had no idea how he would react to her challenge. He might have her thrown out, he might laugh—or he might . . . The silence from the other room was almost deafening at first, then she thought she heard sounds of movement, but she did not dare look round to check.

When his hands descended on her shoulders, she almost cried out in shock because he had approached so noiselessly.

But the arms which slid round her to hold her were bare.

He said with a ghost of laughter in his voice, 'Et maintenant, madame?'

Colour flooded into her face. She said in a muffled voice, 'I—I don't know. I thought—you . . .' She stopped with a little gasp. 'I must have been crazy to come here like this!'

His mouth touched the side of her neck, and trailed small kisses down to the curve of her shoulder. 'Not crazy.' His voice wasn't totally even. 'Just very sweet, ma belle, and very brave.' He paused. 'And what happens next—is this,' he whispered, sliding down the zip of the sundress, and pushing its straps off her shoulders, so that the garment pooled round her feet. 'And this.' Her briefs joined her dress on the floor.

Roche lifted her on to the bed, and lay beside her, his hands cupping her face. He said huskily, 'I want you so much I am almost frightened to touch you.'

Samma wound her arms round his neck. 'I won't break,' she whispered.

'I think I will.' He began to kiss her, his lips brushing hers in a myriad of tiny caresses, each as light as a butterfly's wing. 'Into a million tiny pieces.'

He wooed her slowly and sweetly, his hands exploring with subtle delicacy every line, contour and curve of her body, making each pulse, each nerve-ending sing with joy. His mouth adored her breasts,

teasing each rosy peak into throbbing excitement until
she moaned at the wonder of it.

And against her skin he whispered the kind of
things she had never dreamed she would hear him
say—endearments, small, broken phrases of need and
longing, words that spoke only of love.

The world had shrunk to the compass of his arms.
Nothing existed outside the slow, delicious torment of
yearning he was arousing in her.

She was making explorations of her own, shy at
first, learning the texture of his skin, and the shape of
bone and play of muscle beneath it. As her hands grew
more daring, she felt him tense, his dark face suddenly
strained.

'Don't you like that?' she whispered.

'Too much.' He kissed her deeply, parting her lips
so that his tongue could probe the full sweetness of
her mouth.

She smiled at him, aware of a power she had not
known she possessed. 'Shall I stop?'

'No.' He returned her smile.

For slow, languorous minutes, he let her have her
way, his pleasure in her caresses sighing from his
throat, but when she bent to touch him with her
mouth, he stopped her, his hand tangling in her hair.

'Ah, no,' he told her huskily. 'My control is not
infinite, and I want this first time to be for you, *ma
belle.*'

He kissed the thudding pulse in her throat, and let
his mouth drift downwards over her shoulders and
breasts with a tantalising lack of haste. Samma felt as
if she was being drawn into some inescapable spiral of
sensation, the breath catching in her throat, as
Roche's lips followed the stroke of his fingers down
her pliant body.

She was locked into the spiral now, the ascent to its apex, swift and sharp and quite inevitable. She no longer belonged to herself. She was out of control, her whole being mastered by this torturous ecstasy he was inflicting on her.

Then he lifted himself, moved, and entered her with one fluid thrust. And, as the first scalding wave of pleasure and release welled inside her, she sobbed out his name, and her love for him.

When it was over, they lay for a long time locked in each other's arms, without speaking, kissing a little, touching each other almost with reverence.

At last Samma said, her voice breaking, 'I—I never dreamed it could be like that.'

'Nor I.' Roche wound her hair round his hand and carried it to his lips. 'The first time I saw you,' he said softly, 'you were on the quayside at Cristoforo. You were laughing and your hair was like sunlight. I looked at you and thought—with her, I could begin to live again.' He kissed her mouth. 'After Marie-Christine, I swore that I would use women as she'd used me.' He grimaced. 'But that soon palled. Work, making money, became all in all. I told myself there was no room in my life for love—no need for it.' His hand cupped her breast, stroking it gently. 'How wrong, how stupid could I be?'

Samma nestled her cheek again his shoulder. 'But you were going to send me away.'

'You would never have got on that plane, *ma chère*.' The dark face was serious. 'I would have brought you back—taught you to trust me, somehow.' He kissed the tip of her nose. 'How could you not know I loved you, *ma bien-aimée?*'

'There was Elvire,' she reminded him wryly. 'We were totally at cross purposes there.'

He nodded. 'She is too sensitive about her birth—about the way my father failed to acknowledge her during his lifetime. She begged me to say nothing, to allow you to think she was just the housekeeper. But both of us believed you had guessed or been told the truth about her, and did not approve.'

'Who could have told me?'

'Liliane Duvalle, perhaps. God knows, she spent enough time on my family's private affairs to have discovered that Elvire was my sister. Or Marie-Christine might have hinted something to her.'

'So many secrets.' Samma touched her lips to his skin. 'Learning to trust is a two-way process, *mon amour.*'

'I know,' he said remorsefully. 'But I was so afraid of losing you, Samantha. After all, you made it clear you had agreed to my proposal for Solange's sake only. How could I confess she was not really my daughter, or even hint at the other problems you might encounter? You might never have married me, and I could not risk that.'

'And if I had turned you down?'

'Then I would probably have taken a leaf out of *Le Diable's* book, and carried you off anyway.' He brushed her mouth with his. 'As I'd have done at the airport tomorrow. But fortunately you needed me, *mon coeur,* although not, *hélas,* in the way I wanted you.'

She sighed. 'I thought you wanted to sleep me with me because I was—there. A—a temporary diversion.'

'If you'd examined the papers you signed last night, *ma belle,* you would have realised my plans for us were totally permanent.' He brushed a strand of sweat-dampened hair back from her forehead very tenderly. 'Why did you suddenly turn on me like that?'

She bit her lip. 'The same thing, I suppose. A—fear of being used—without love.'

'Ah, *mignonne,* why do you think, in the end, I walked

away from you last night? Because I could not take you with anger between us.'

She said, 'You walked away once before, when I went to your room and waited for you in bed.'

His mouth twisted. 'I had been at the casino, *ma belle*, trying to drown my sorrows, and the memory of our quarrel in alcohol. When I got to my room, I thought at first I was seeing things. Then, when I realised you were really there, I had to come to terms with the fact that I was in no fit state to make love to you.'

'And all those other nights, when you didn't come to bed?'

'I drove around—sometimes to the beach, or slept on the couch in my study. I always took care the servants never saw me. Or Solange.'

Samma traced a pattern on his chest with one finger. 'About Solange—it's not enough, Roche, to take responsibility for her. She needs more than that from you.' She looked at him soberly. 'Whatever her mother was, she needs warmth and affection, openly expressed.'

'That is something you will have to teach me, *mon ange*. I have become used to—hiding my feelings, or pretending they do not exist.'

'Really?' Samma stretched lithely against him, delighting in the responsive stir of his flesh. 'I would never have guessed.'

'Beware, *madame*.' He gave her a ferocious frown. 'You provoke me at your peril!'

Samma pouted in mock-alarm. 'What are you threatening me with, *monsieur*? The Delacroix curse?'

Roche laughed out loud. 'My own personal version,' he whispered, and began to kiss her again.

YOU'RE INVITED TO ACCEPT **FOUR ROMANCES** AND A TOTE BAG **FREE!**

Acceptance card

ROMANCE

Next month's romances from Mills & Boon

Each month, you can choose from a world of variety in romance with Mills & Boon. These are the new titles to look out for next month.

VILLAIN OF THE PIECE Catherine George
THE LATIMORE BRIDE Emma Goldrick
THE VERANCHETTI MARRIAGE Lynne Graham
SNOWFIRE Dana James
THE LOVING GAMBLE Flora Kidd
CENTREFOLD Valerie Parv
THE BITTER TASTE OF LOVE Lilian Peake
MAN OF STONE Frances Roding
STORM CLOUDS GATHERING Edwina Shore
LOVE'S WRONGS Angela Wells
A SHADOWED LOVE Rachel Ford
YESTERDAY'S ENEMY Lee Stafford
MOWANA MAGIC Margaret Way
HOT PURSUIT Karen Van Der Zee

Buy them from your usual paperback stockist, or write to: Mills & Boon Reader Service, P.O. Box 236, Thornton Rd, Croydon, Surrey CR9 3RU, England. Readers in Southern Africa — write to: Independent Book Services Pty, Postbag X3010, Randburg, 2125, S. Africa.

Mills & Boon
the rose of romance

GA

SPOT THE COUPLE
AND WIN A
£1,000
REAL PEARL NECKLACE
PLUS 10 PAIRS OF REAL PEARL EAR STUDS WORTH OVER £100 EACH

A

B

No piece of jewellery is more romantic than the soft glow and lustre of a real pearl necklace, pearls that grow mysteriously from a grain of sand to a jewel that has a romantic history that can be traced back to Cleopatra and beyond.

To enter just study Photograph A showing a young couple. Then look carefully at Photograph B showing the same section of the river. Decide where you think the couple are standing and mark their position with a cross in pen.

Complete the entry form below and mail your entry PLUS TWO OTHER "SPOT THE COUPLE" Competition Pages from June, July or August Mills and Boon paperbacks, to Spot the Couple, Mills and Boon Limited, Eton House, 18/24 Paradise Road, Richmond, Surrey, TW9 1SR, England. All entries must be received by December 31st 1988.

ENTRY FORM

Name _____

Address _____

_____

I bought this book in TOWN _____ COUNTRY _____

This offer applies only to books purchased outside the UK & Eire.
You may be mailed with other offers as a result of this application.